Re-visions

Stories from Stories

Meredith Sue Willis

Re-visions

Stories from Stories

By Meredith Sue Willis

Fic
Wil

Copyright 2011
Meredith Sue Willis

Library of Congress Cataloging-in-Publication Data
Willis, Meredith Sue.
Revisions : stories from stories / by Meredith Sue Willis.
p. cm.
ISBN-13: 978-0-9801786-6-1 (alk. paper)
ISBN-10: 0-9801786-6-5 (alk. paper)
I. Title.
PS3573.I45655R48 2011
813'.54--dc22

2010006694

Hamilton Stone Editions
P.O. Box 43
Maplewood, NJ 07040
Web site: http://www.hamiltonstone.org
Email: hstone@hamiltonstone.org

Acknowledgments

"The Adventure of Scheherezade and Dunzyad" was published in *The Pedestal Magazine*, April 21 - June 21, 2005 issue (http://www.thepedestalmagazine.com/gallery.php?item=1830).

"Baucis and Philemon # 3" appeared in a barely recognizable version as "Baucis and Philemon" in *Epoch*, Winter, 1973, pp. 177-183.

"The Great Wolf" was first published in *Earth's Daughters 25/26: Another Comforter*, 1985.

"Her Statue" first appeared as "The Icon" in *Libera*, Summer, 1975.

"Claribel, Queen of Tunis, and Antonio the Usurper of Milan" was first published in *The Little Magazine*, Volume Twelve, Numbers One and Two, spring-summer, 1978.

"Legend of the Locust Root" was published as "Miracle of the Locust Root" in *Kentucky Writing*, Vol. 6, No. 2, Spring/Summer 1991 and then as part of *In the Mountains of America* (Mercury House, 1994).

"Martha, Sister of Lazarus" first appeared in *Story Quarterly 7/8*, 1978.

"Miss Topsy" was published in *Other Voices 18*, Spring 1993.

"Sermon of the Younger Monica" was first published in *West Branch 11*, 1982.

This book is dedicated to people who still read
Ovid, *Uncle Tom's Cabin*, and the Bible.

Other Books
By Meredith Sue Willis

Novels and Stories
A Space Apart
Higher Ground
Only Great Changes
Quilt Pieces (with Jane Wilson Joyce)
In the Mountains of America
Trespassers
Oradell at Sea
Dwight's House and Other Stories
The City Built of Starships
Out of the Mountains

Novels for Children
The Secret Super Powers of Marco
Marco's Monster
Billie of Fish House Lane

Nonfiction about Writing
Personal Fiction Writing
Blazing Pencils
Deep Revision
Ten Strategies to Write Your Novel

Re-visions

Stories from Stories

Table of Contents

Sermon of the Younger Monica....................................13

Martha, Sister of Lazarus 25

Legend of the Locust Root................................41

Dunzyad, Scheherezade, and the King............................45

Her Statue..59

The Great Wolf..67

Baucis and Philemon # 3..................................79

Claribel Queen of Tunis 89

Miss Topsy..105

A Note On the Sources....................................119

Sermon of the Younger Monica

Sermon of the Younger Monica

As a child, I stole no pears. I was the pear that was stolen. I am here now, my children, to declare that we are all pears hanging by a fragile stem above our destruction. The sun shines, we are watered, we flower, and we fruit.

Then the Vandals cut us down. They took Hippo where Augustine died as Bishop. They will take Carthage as well. In some days in some places you would not have to know this– that the Vandals always come. I didn't know it in the flush of my health and youth, but in this city at this time, you know it. What I am here to tell you is the other part.

The only home I remember is the house where I was taken to be a handmaiden. All the great families used to take in girl children, give them light work, raise them in the family so that the sons would not be driven to the women of the waterfront when they reached their manhood. The youngest son of the family was my special charge. I slept in his bed to warm him and I played with him and wiped his nose if it ran. I was his handmaiden, and one day I might be his concubine or even his third or fourth wife. I was content with my fortune.

Then Augustine of Hippo came to teach the sons of our family. He was no bishop yet, of course, nor even a Christian, but they say his mother, Saint Monica to be, was even then in Thagaste praying hourly for his conversion. He was already well known as a rhetorician, and he taught for a living. Our family would have permitted him to do even less teaching for the prestige of having a prize winning classicist attached to the household, but he took his teaching seriously; he made a sincere effort, gathering those cheerful wild boys into the atrium every day for lessons. I would work around them, plucking off dead flowers, feeding the caged birds. I was of an age when I noticed the beauty of men, but I admired the young professor from afar, as girls sigh from rooftops over the conquering general's triumph.

One hot day when the boys were being stupid, gazing at the sky making bird calls, doing anything but attending, the teacher lost his temper: "Look, donkey heads, look at the little handmaiden. Even she listens better than you do." He made me recite a passage from the story of Aeneas. I had been emptying seed husks and fruit rinds from the cages, and I had absorbed the lines without effort. "Do you see?" he said to the boys. "Do you see how easy it is? If even a girl servant can parrot it, surely the scions of a great family of Carthage can manage to squash a few lines in through their ears."

I got pinches from the big boys, but I worked that night with my little master so that the next day I could listen proudly as he recited. It never occurred to me that in the famous man's eyes I was hanging at the end of a branch, dangling before his lips full and blush pink. I thought I was cleaning bird cages, and all the time I was tempting Augustine.

You see, in his boyhood, it was not stealing the pears he regretted, but the wanting, the greed. He fought the sin of theft less than the sin of desiring what was not his. When he could fight his desire no longer, he fell upon the pears, ripped them from the trees, gorged himself until he was bloated and humiliated. Thus one midday when the family was off observing their rites at the temple, I went into the atrium and came upon the teacher of rhetoric, leaning against a tree with his chin pulled to one side, and all the ligaments of his neck straining. I thought he was having a fit.

"Order me!" I cried. "Do you want wine? Is there a medication in your pouch?"

But he could not speak. He had never spoken to me, had only spoken at me that once, and he did not speak now, but seized me with his graceful scholar's arms, pressed me to his chest. He spoke many words then, words of fruit and passion, biting his teeth into my shoulder, lifting up my breasts and sucking them. He quoted from the classics about Dido and Helen. He held me tighter, and I could feel him swelling under his clothes, and then he cried out and threw himself on a couch, sobbing. I had no idea why: I thought it was a fit after all, or perhaps possession by a demon. I ran for wine, which he drank, and then went off without speaking, rearranging the front of his robe.

For three days he did not come to teach, and on the fourth morning I was summoned where I had never been before, to the small receiving chamber of our paterfamilias. He winked and gave me as kiss. "You're still so small," he said. "Not really developed yet. Is my youngest boy good?"

"Oh, the best!" I said. "He's the sweetest child who ever lived," and then, thinking that the great man would rather hear how strong his son was, I added, "But very manly. He commands me like a general."

"Are you fond of him then? And will you be sorry when you have to part with him?" I went cold, thinking the boy was to be sent away to Rome. My master said, "It's too bad to take you from him, but our young teacher of rhetoric has offered me money for you. He wants to set you up in a little house as a legal concubine. Do you understand how unusual this is? That your future is secure?" He went on and on about what an opportunity this was, how the most accomplished hetaeras of twenty would boast of such an offer, and women of thirty would poison their sisters for it. All I could think was that I was being sent away from my little boy who would do anything I told him, from the house with all the people in my world. That I was being sent off with a madman.

I knew nothing. I was thirteen years old. I knew birds and boys and the fat servants of an easy, affluent household. I

15

knew nothing of how to organize a house or command others. For that was the height to which he raised me. I was, in legal language on papers I marked myself, guaranteed my freedom should I be set aside by the teacher of rhetoric, and furthermore, granted the small house in perpetuity. All this for such service as any woman provides her man or master, for seeing to food and clean tunics. For sharing his bed.

People believed in security in those days, my children. We believed the future could be assured by a small stone house with a garden, by a supply of linen and crockery, by couscous in the pot, honey in jars.

And yet I was like one taken from the garden of Eden. I felt myself imprisoned in a place populated by enemies. The servants in my little house looked on me as an interloper. He never knew that, but he realized quickly enough how ignorant I was. I didn't know how to do so much as measure out lamp oil or order meals. I became sick and lost weight. I cowered in bed, convinced that at any moment I would be turned out naked in the street. I did not understand the papers I'd marked, nor did I understand him. By nature he was a kind man. Once he realized my ignorance, he searched the city and found an elder lady, a former concubine herself, now living in comfort, who came to me and showed me how to order from the market, and how to reweave a tear in linen. How to speak to servants. He instructed me, too, showing me where to put his clean tunics, taking me to the pavilion in the garden that he used for a study and showing me how to grind his inks and arrange his scrolls. He taught me passages of the classics that he found appropriate to my light voice and ordered me to recite during his meals. He was in all things eager for my comfort. And yet, I think if I had not been of strong country stock and well nourished from my old house, that I would have died the first year. Not so much from pining, though I grieved for my little master, but from thinking I had turned into something monstrous.

For I seemed to cause him pain. He still had his fits. He would kindly instruct me in the morning and then, perhaps in the middle of the afternoon when I was working on some sewing, he would cross the garden from his study, come to the chamber where I was and lean against the wall as he had that first time, straining his face, sometimes cursing, and then he would burst the bonds of restraint and come at me, carry me to the bed. I thought these events were a deferred punishment for some error– that I had made his breakfast porridge too hot, that I had let his ink dry out. I am not saying he abused me– he was the one who seemed abused: he appeared to suffer from my presence.

After a while, of course, I became used to it, and I decided that my body, or parts of my body, had power over him. He addressed the parts of me: O little foot, he would say. O silken breast. I began to believe there was something in all this. That I had the power to summon him and disturb his serenity. I experimented, wearing special pink sea shells in my earlobes, dabbing perfume in the whorls of my ears and stroking kohl around the eyes. Sometimes I would sit in the garden near his study with all my odors and veils and will him to come to me. When he came at last, I would flush with pride and think I was what he called me in his fits– a seductress, a phenomenon of nature.

I know better now. The great man was a scholar, and they sit too much. The blood pools in their loins and must be dissipated. It is a matter of health. I only began to understand the summer I became pregnant. I had left off earrings and kohl that summer, hoping he would leave me alone. My feet were swollen with heat and I had an aching tooth. I hid in the kitchen with the cook, but he still came for me. He cursed me sometimes for tempting him at this time when it might endanger our child, and I said For the love of God then stay away from me. But he said I was drawing him to me with the swell of my belly and the sway of my buttocks. The scales fell from my eyes; I saw that I was doing nothing, that there was only his lust.

Yet the time of my mistaken pride was not over. I thought the birth of Adeodatus earned me a place, a name. I thought I would be like the other Monica, his mother, the saint. I had always believed that the reason he never used my name was that it seemed to him improper to call his concubine by his mother's name. He didn't like to speak of her to me at all, but after Adeo was born, I begged for stories about how she had raised him. He would tell me of the pain in her beautiful eyes when he was greedy, of the gentleness in her voice when she remonstrated. I thought I would learn to be such a Monica by hearing the stories. I would imagine as I held Adeo and pulled his outstretched fingers from the spiny flowers that I was the first Monica saying No, no, little August, with stern but loving eyes.

Then Monica herself came. She came when least expected like Christos the bridegroom, on an ordinary day. He had gone out to talk philosophy with his Manichean friends, and I was laying Adeo in the crib. One of the servants ran in saying "Miss, Miss, a litter is coming with a lady from across the desert!" I guessed at once who it was. My legs were weak, but my head was clear. I said, "Set up a divan and pillows in the garden. Prepare fruit drinks and a foot bath and send for the cleanest boy you can find in the market to work a fan." I seized my best head scarf and ran out into the street to meet her.

She was as beautiful and calm as I had imagined: the large lustrous eyes, the dark hair silvered. I had not expected so many rings, however, or the gold threads in the embroidery in her clothes. They said the Christians were people to whom the goods of this world meant nothing, so I supposed all these things were so common to her that she did not even notice that she was wearing them.

She looked at me, and spoke as if to an invisible lady beside her: "This must be the concubine."

18

"I am your servant, madam," I said, but I added, "I am the mother of Adeodatus."

"The mother of Adeodatus." She allowed us to lift her from the litter. She allowed us to take her inside, and to give her a clean robe, to wash her feet. I watched the fine eyes to see if our arrangements satisfied her. I made a great show of rejecting the market boy for being dusty and sending for another one and then moving the new one ten times to be sure his fan brought the coolest air scented by the lime trees. She chose a drink. She selected fruit. She asked for Adeo, who was brought sleeping and she sent him back till he woke. She wanted to see where her son studied. At last, when she had examined everything— baby, garden, the quality of the clean robe I gave her— she looked at me again. "You seem a simple girl," she said. "Even a good girl. You seem to do your duty and yet they tell me you have enthralled my son. That he will consider no marriages because of you. Do you use magic from the jungle people beyond the desert? Ancient Egyptian love philtres?"

I said, "Lady, your son is a most generous man respected far and wide, and he is my master. But he is the slave of his own passion and I happened to be the one he saw when the blood was running most hotly in his loins."

She seemed to sip of me as of her fruit drink then. "We'll make a Christian of you," she said. "When you and my son are no longer in a state of sin." I forgave her all the testing and tasting. I wanted her to take me and Adeo far away, to drink us in, to let us live in the folds of her fine garments. I would have done anything to be with her, although I think she was not truly a saint but one gifted by nature to calm people with her soothing presence. I loved her, not knowing that she would be the instrument of the greatest wrong ever done me.

She was for the next several years kind, sending gifts, personally checking the papers I had signed to be sure I would be provided for once she got her son away. She had a cousin in Carthage who agreed to be my guardian, to find me a

19

husband when the time came. I agreed to all this, even told Augustine he should go to Rome when she got him the promise of an appointment. He went, and I felt I had done right. I was ready to become a Christian, if she wanted that. But the wrong she did me– the wrong they did me together– was to take away my son, to make me not even the mother of Adeodatus anymore. I wished later that they had taken him when he was an infant, because then I loved him with my breasts and my belly. But they took him after I had taught him, lived with him, centered my days around him. They took him after I loved him with my soul. Monica came and said this venture would be the making of Adeo, and she took him to Italy to live with her and the bishop-to-be. She didn't lie to me; she said it would be years at best before I would see him again, and then she left: left me my freedom, my house, and no name at all.

Thus the first lesson I have already told you, my children: that the nothing is inalienable. That the Vandals come to all our lives. Every woman's son is ripped from her arms; all city gates are battered down; all avenues overrun. Sometimes the Vandals have the fine eyes of saints; sometimes the assassin is a little fruit seller in the marketplace. But the Vandals always come.

I let them get me a husband, set me up in my dried fruit business in Augustine's old study. I had news of what they were doing in Italy: of Augustine's great conversion, the devotion of his mother Monica, the precocity of Adeo. And then I heard of the fever that took the boy. That Adeo and Monica were both gone, I would never see either of them again. I became bitter in my heart. I continued as you have known me, selling fruit, doing my duty to my good man, but having no more children. I would not have children. I adopted market urchins and the handmaidens with bad skin that no one would buy. I lived a righteous life, but carried a special pocket of hate for the only one of them left, for Augustine. I promised myself an outcome, a climax.

When he at last returned to Africa, it was as Bishop of Hippo, and I bought a dagger. I kept it ready, and on the day he came to the basilica of Carthage to speak to us, I held it deep in my garments and went to hear him with everyone else. He was thicker and grayer, softer than I remembered, and not nearly so tall. It seemed that he and I had at last come to resemble one another: both broad with a wide stance on the earth, people who call others our children, since we lost our own. After his sermon, he came down among the people, and they surged and called out to him and tried to touch him. Father! they said, Saint! But no one shoved me. I stood my ground, respected by those around me, even as he was. No one guessed I had a dagger hidden in my garments. I stood where I was till he passed near me, and then I called out too. "Augustine!" I said. He hesitated, he turned. I said, "Augustine! Do you know me?"

And he said, with the gentleness and kindness which were always his nature, "It's Monica. It's my little Monica."

They were filling the space between us, importuning him, tugging at his robes. He called, "Before I go back to Hippo— come and see me— I want to tell you about the boy!"

I allowed the dagger to drop. Let there be rumors of assassination by the Pelagrians, I thought. I have no reason to hate this man. He loved Adeo and he loved his mother and he knows my name.

This, then, is the second lesson, my children. Call each other by name. Christ may know your name, let that be as it may, but say each other's names. Call your children by name and your neighbors. Call your servants and the beggar in the marketplace by name. And the Vandals too, if you can pronounce them.

Give no titles of honor.

Let my name be Monica.

Martha,
Sister of Lazarus

Martha, Sister of Lazarus

First I was proud of the prosperity of my family and that my brother Lazarus could spend his days studying holy scripture. Then I was proud of the tents my sister Mary and I wove that were so fine a proconsul of Rome sent his majordomo to buy one. I used to keep a little store in the courtyard too. I had my own recipe for black olives cured in wine and I kept stacks of oranges and lemons and citrons from our own garden. Now my garden is as hard as stone because the new-law Jews squat there. And nothing comes from my looms but coarse cloth woven quickly for a profit.

They always tease me and say, "Consider the lilies of the field, Martha, they don't weave tent-cloth."

And I reply, "He told us to give all we have to the poor. If we don't have, we can't give."

I am also in charge of the giveaway: I'm the one who has to face the smirking widows with the torn veils they're too lazy to mend. Their insolent children yell, "Hey lady my mother is the poorest, that means we get our bread first, doesn't it?" And I pass out the bread, and I bake it and knead it and grind the wheat while Mary and Lazarus and all the others wait for the Nazarene, singing about how he gave everything for us, even the breath from his body.

Well, it is my pride to give everything I have too, my baking, my weaving, my sweat.

It seems to me that we have been waiting for the Nazarene and talking about his coming for too long.

Months before he visited Bethany it was the Nazarene this, the Nazarene that, the Nazarene told this story. They said he healed a leper and got drunk with a tax collector. He wore his hair long and didn't take a wife, but harlots traveled in his company. He was the biggest news since the proconsul bought the tent. Down at the synagogue Lazarus and his cronies were pretty sure the man was a religious phenomenon and they sent a representative to question him.

"Spies you mean," I said, just to tease. I always tease Lazarus. When I was a girl I used to be jealous of all the care he got when he was sick, but there came a time when I realized that I was the one who bought him his time to study and memorize and quote scripture and I became proud of him then and said, Go study Lazarus, come home and complain that I work on the Sabbath; nothing you say bothers me because the hours of your days belong to me.

But that was before the Nazarene took everyone's days.

One evening Lazarus brought three friends home with him. He started saying Woman this and Woman that and Woman where is the wine? I said to him right in front of the others, Lazarus, you don't have a wife. Fetch your own wine. But then I had them sit in the garden, and I gave them wine and laid out a feast too. I sent Mary with plates of food. Her cheeks got redder and her eyes got bigger. "They say they have positive proof he is the Messiah," she said. "They say he is of the house of David."

"So claim half the families in Bethany," I said.

Lazarus wanted to talk to me, and I came, out into the garden. My garden was like a rich man's that night with the orange of the lamps and the odor of citron. "We have extended an invitation," Lazarus said. "We have invited the new rabbi to come and speak in Bethany and this house has been chosen to receive him." The men smiled and nodded in unison.

I said, "And how many am I expected to feed in this ramshackle hut without so much as a servant?"

"All the women will pitch in," said Lazarus too quickly, because he was afraid I was going to embarrass him again.

I gave him my evil eye for a few seconds, then said, "Well, Lazarus, you know I love a party."

People were generous for the reception. They brought bread dough and apricot paste and platters of stuffed grape leaves and meatballs in gravy. The wine merchant gave me a key to his storeroom and said to help myself if we ran short. I put out scented oil and linen for the guests to wipe away their travel dust, and I told Mary to make sure no one but the Nazarene himself should use one particular napkin, woven by our mother, the best I had. While I talked to her she moved up and down on her toes, bracelets jiggling and jingling, and I wasn't sure she heard a thing. Then Lazarus came whining that there weren't enough pillows for the Nazarene's people. "Let them sit on their heels," I said. "They've given up worldly comfort, haven't they?" But of course I sent Mary to borrow pillows.

I knew exactly when the Nazarene entered the house because everyone went running out of my kitchen and poured into the garden, stretching their necks to see. A man I had never seen was standing on the balustrade and I grabbed him by the hood of his cloak and dragged him off. "Whose house do you think this is?" I said to him, but he just yelled in my face, "Did you see him? Did you see him?" I caught a glimpse then of a man, not too tall, with a glistening river of wavy hair. I was struck by how completely without knots or tangles it was. I had heard that the harlots who traveled with him brushed and oiled it twice a day. Something in its unnatural smoothness disturbed me, and I went back to the kitchen. Not a person came to help me while he was speaking, not a woman, not a child, not my brother or sister. I could hear his voice, but not what he was saying. I kneaded crushed wheat into ground lamb and stuffed vegetables, but the voice spread through my kitchen, penetrated the odors of raw meat and heating oil, touched the back of my neck.

I finally went out myself to pass wine. People were sitting all through the house, on the porch, in the garden in the sun. They had become still and calm as they listened to him. He was on a bench under the lemon tree, his hair spread over his shoulders like a garment. I might have sat down and listened if it had not been for Mary. She was hunkering on the ground closer to him than Lazarus or the study house men or even his own people. She had laid my finest linen napkin on the dirt at his feet and was pouring the fabulously expensive Damascene oil in a basin to wash his feet. And she used her own naked hair to wipe his toes. This is where he gets his harlots, I thought. He steals younger sisters from decent families and turns them into camp followers for that gang of Galileans. I ran back to the kitchen, to do anything to work up a sweat. And all the time the voice was on me too, in my ears, and on my shoulders and back, touching me everywhere.

After a while there was a let-up of tension and people were with me again, picking up platters of food. "Weren't you there, Martha?" they said. "Didn't you hear him?" No mention of Mary's brazen behavior, so I thought perhaps Nazarene had enacted a true miracle and fastened down the tongues of the Bethany gossips.

I said, "The way they're drinking wine out there, they'll believe anything the man says."

The women gasped and covered their mouths. I turned around and saw that the Nazarene himself was standing in the doorway.

"I don't care," I said. "I talk too much, anybody will tell you that, but I don't care. I don't think you're the Messiah, I think you're preaching for free meals." The women were shocked, the Nazarene smiled, and I felt sick at my stomach, but kept on talking. "All these hours my sister sits in there with you while I haven't left this overheated kitchen except once to pour wine for your thirsty friends. No one thinks how much effort goes into all this cooking. Not to mention the cleaning we have to do yet and Mary hasn't lifted a finger since you got here except to shame herself by washing your feet with her hair."

"Ah, Martha," he spoke softly, just for me. "Mary has chosen the good part. I wouldn't take that away from her."

"The good part you say! Getting drunk and playing with your feet?"

The neighbors buzzed, thinking I had gone too far, but he said mildly to them, "Leave me alone with my sister Martha."

I said, "Now you've made a fool of me and Mary too. When do you take my poor brother's dignity?"

The Nazarene sat down on a covered jar and leaned against the wall, propping one leg on his knee. He sighed, and his head dropped to one side. He had fallen asleep, just that quickly. Well, I thought, that is some kind of distinction, to talk the Nazarene to sleep. I walked closer to get a good look at him. He had a sturdy leg covered with silky brown hair. I heard voices in the passageway, some of his coarse friends, and I stopped them at the door. "Your master is taking a nap. Go and get drunk and let him rest."

They were smirking. "Are you Martha? Your sister Mary is beating a tambourine and dancing."

"Go away, Galileans," I said. "You smell like fish. Fish cooked in wine that has sat out too long."

I pulled a stool into the doorway where I could watch the passageway and him too. I thought about strangers wandering all over my house, picking my fruit, trampling the rugs, stealing from my chests. I knew it was happening, but I just pulled my knees up and stared at the last orange light falling on the wall above his head, leaving his face in shadow.

His leg dropped to the floor suddenly, and he stood up and stretched.

I got up too. "Now you expect to be fed, I suppose."

"Have you been watching so that no one disturbs me, Martha? You have such kindness in you," he said, and when I started making noises of protest, he raised a hand. "Sit down, Martha, I think you need someone to feed you."

Then he put his hands on my upper arms and turned me around, backed me to the jar he had sat on and made me sit on it. I could feel the warmth under me where he had been, and where his hands had pressed my arms. He tore open a bread and dumped in meatballs and rice and gravy and pickles and poured me a big cup of wine. He put the wine cup in my left hand and the stuffed bread in my right. Then he served himself and came and stood in front of me as if he wanted to be sure I didn't run away until I had finished eating.

I had been hungry. My food served by him was delicious.

"What else can I do for you, Martha?" he said.

"Don't take my sister."

"I don't take anything, I give."

"Don't give anything to my sister then."

He touched my knee. "And you, Martha? Don't you want to be a part of it too?" Then he touched my knee again, with all his fingers, knew the shape of it. He had a way of seeming puzzled, surprised by such a thing as a knee.

I couldn't move away and I couldn't hide the quickening of my breath. If he had wanted me then in that way, if he had broken his famous vows, I would have gone to him like a lamb. All through the house there was a buzzing of locusts eating and I thought that in the morning the man would be gone and the house littered with dry insect corpses and blackened cloth and broken pottery, charred by his passing.

I said, "You are burning me."

He laid both palms on my legs. "Burn then," he said. "Be a lamp against the darkness."

"I will not," I said, and closed my eyes and did not move.

"Do not be afraid of burning," he murmured, and I pressed my lips tight together so I would not even speak, and I stayed that way until he gave a small laugh and lifted his hands.

Then they came for him. He had to travel on, they said.

I stayed where I was, assessing the damage. Later I would see what they had done to my house, but first I had to see what he had done to me.

He was not like us, or else he would not have burnt thumb prints into my arms and my knee. Or else he would not through that touch have left a thing growing in me, a demon, a man-shaped baby of fire fastened between my loins. I thought that, if I moved, the air would set me off flames in me like tinder. But I thwarted him. I did not move, and I blackened within rather than burst into his flames.

Mary wanted to burn. I am the Moth, she said, and He is the Light. My Master is a Great Flame of Light.! I locked the house to keep her from running away. Lazarus, on the other hand, was tortured by the Nazarene. At his synagogue there was a war between the ones who thought the Nazarene was the Messiah and those who didn't. Lazarus could not choose sides and couldn't bear uncertainty either. He decided to go and try to get the Nazarene to explain again.

I said, "Go, but don't bring him back to this house."

Lazarus was gone for a month and came back fifteen pounds lighter with a fever. He talked all the time I was putting him to bed. "The Nazarene won't answer," he whispered, "He says we've heard the message. He says now is the time to forsake father and mother, brother and sister, and follow him."

"I'm glad you have more sense," I said, but I was mistaken.

Lazarus did not rest, but wrote. He tried to get down every word he had heard the Nazarene say, every little story, every sermon. "I can't remember," he would mutter. "I can't remember."

Then, still ill, he dressed and went out like a wounded old dog with no teeth who still limps out after the bitch in heat.

I said, "But he's going farther and farther from Bethany. The whole lot of them is going to be arrested any day now, you said so yourself. And you're still sick."

"Now I know the question to ask," he said.

I said, "He says whatever comes to his mind. It makes sense only if you want it to make sense."

Coughing in the chill dawn, Lazarus said, "He is inspired. The words are surely inspired, but whether he is the One, I have to hear more."

Mary tried to go with him, of course, and I held her with my arm across her chest. She shouted, "Tell my Master that there is no light but his!"

The second time Lazarus came back, it was tied to a peddler's donkey, in delirium. He had slips of paper hidden all through his clothes and he kept patting at himself and saying, "Every word, this time I got every word."

Mary said, "Lazarus wants to put the Light into a little lantern."

I said, "I would like to make a bonfire and burn every word the Nazarene ever said and see how that lights up Judea."

Lazarus was sicker than I had ever seen him before. All night I would wring out damp cloths for his forehead and comb his beard and feed him broth. And always, his raving. Out of his weakness would come a burst of strength and he would sit up and beg me to bring the Nazarene. Sometimes he uttered a single word over and over in different voices: "Love and light and light and love and love and light," he said, and then said the words backward and counted the letters and added and multiplied.

There was no doubt of the Nazarene's power. I was on guard all the time against the demon he left in me. It especially liked the lamplight and shadows in Lazarus's sick room. It would grown large and tried to lie across my body, but I would spring to my feet and rearrange the pillows or bathe Lazarus' face. As soon as I rested, though, it began to moan in my ear again.

Meanwhile, I sent messages. Twice I hired a boy to go to the Nazarene and tell him Lazarus of Bethany is desperately ill and desires your presence. Dear Physician, I made them promise to add. The Nazarene sent back messages:

I weep for Lazarus my brother; I send Love. But he never came.

And one night Lazarus sat up sobbing and choked on some word the Nazarene taught him, and clawed for breath, and then died.

I watched him go, and was overwhelmed by the stillness.

Lazarus's funeral was the last propriety ever observed in our house. We put the body in the cave and the stones on the lid, and mourners came down and I made sure they were served more food than they could eat in a week.

Then I went out and squatted on the porch and looked at the garden. The next day I sat again; I had never gone so long without working. I watched a lizard on the wall. Summer dust blew onto the porch and into the house. I did not wet it down and sweep it out, but let it slip in like a fellow mourner. I fancied that the dust might be Lazarus's dust.

On the fourth day, Mary's sandals came through the dust. "Prepare for the Bridegroom," she said, and she walked out of the house.

I ran into the street after her, and the force of the sun staggered me. People asked where we were going at noon?

"The Bridegroom is coming!" cried Mary.

"We must stop him!" I cried.

"Who?" they cried. "Who must we stop?" And they followed after us, people dizzy with me from the heat. At the top of the hill we could see the clouds and the knot of men moving in unison, the caravan with no baggage, the Nazarene's locusts. I picked up speed, I lunged ahead of Mary. I would have plunged right through the hairy Galileans, the wild eyed zealots, the money keepers and harlots, but they closed ranks and snarled when they saw me.

"I am the bucket of water!" I screamed. "Where is the Flame?"

He came out and showed himself to me, looking not like a flame at all this time. There was a ratsnest in his hair, and he looked smaller, but I could still feel it, that he could do what he wanted with us.

"Take Mary, then, " I said. "She wants to go with you. But leave me alone."

"I've come for Lazarus," he said.

"You've come too late. He's dead."

"This is the right time. Where is he lying?"

"In his tomb! Aren't you a Jew? He was in his tomb by sunset."

The Nazarene turned to his horde. "We go to the tomb of Lazarus of Bethany."

The guards tried to push me aside, but I pushed back. "Nazarene, it's been too many days, he already stinks!" The crowd started to move, growling in its excitement, back down the hill into Bethany and then up the steps to the graveyard. All the way in front, in front of the Nazarene himself, was Mary sweeping the steps with her hair before he walked on them.

He addressed us from the mouth of the cave. He seemed to be talking about birds, but I never was able to hear the words of his sermons. I think it was about birds because he shaped flying things in the air with his hands that seemed to pluck at fruit, to drop seeds.

I began to be aware of odors. I could smell everything in that windy place: the perfume Mary wore, the sour breath of the wine-seller and the lactation of a Bethany woman. One of the disciples had rotting teeth. I smelled what people had eaten for lunch, and their feet and their clothes, and I smelled the stale bones and dust of the dead.

Under it all, the rot of death.

The Nazarene himself had no odor. He was a blank at the mouth of the cave. Around him seeped the other odor, the breakdown of my salves and oils, the opening of what should have stayed sealed.

34

I thought, if this man can do this thing, if this man can do this, then we should turn him over to the Romans.

Lazarus was coming out of the cave. Hardly able to walk for the tightness of the grave linen. "This is an abomination," I said. I wished I had wrapped him tighter. Awkwardly he scratched his throat, his crotch.

The Nazarene's followers were the most shocked: they thought they knew what he could do, but this rocked them. The people of Bethany, though, were happy to believe. The eyes of Bethany were awestruck and delighted.

"Hosanna!" shrieked Mary, and a man began to sob and tear his clothes.

Lazarus tugged at a piece of binding so his eyes were both uncovered, then his mouth. He blinked, he looked around, he said to me, "I itch."

"Get your master to scratch you," I said. "Where is he, where is the grave robber?"

I didn't see him anywhere. I pounded a disciple on the back until we got a robe for Lazarus's nakedness and then I unwound him. The odor made me retch, and also the damp white corrugations of his skin, huge patches flaking off with the bandages and the new skin underneath raw and shiny pink. The robe kept slipping off, showing his graveyard leprosy. I told him to close his mouth so we wouldn't have to smell his breath, but he was still feverish. He needed to talk to someone about something very important, he said.

The rest of them didn't need the Nazarene: the whole crowd, Bethany, hairy Galileans, all of them were clapping and laughing. Mary grabbed Lazarus by the wrist. "Dance, brother!" she cried. And he lifted one foot, and after a while the other and everyone cheered and followed him and Mary out of that place.

Everyone but me, and then I realized the Nazarene hadn't gone either. The Nazarene was leaning against a rock by the side of the cave mouth with his arms spread as far as he could reach. There were lines as deep as scars in his cheeks.

"They want the miracles," I said, "Not your light, if you really have any."

He turned a cheek to the stone, let his head drop down as it would at the end.

"Did they understand?" he asked.

"They understand that there's nothing they fear more than death. They understand they'll do anything not to die."

He nodded.

I said, "I smelled everything, every man and woman in the place living and dead. You smell us all the time, don't you? You smell me right now– " I covered my mouth.

He let his arms relax, then his body. He slid down to sit on the ground. "That's nothing," he said. "Smelling is nothing. Let me lay my head on your lap a little while."

"You brought my brother back and his fever isn't even cured."

"I'll cure his fever later. That's nothing."

"Everything is nothing to you," I said, but I sat down and let him put his head on my lap, and I worked at the ratsnest in his hair. "Where are your handmaidens, Nazarene? Is your head too heavy for them now?"

He said, "This body won't be with you much longer. It will go, and come back, but not stay long."

"I believe that. When the priests and the Romans hear you're raising the dead."

His head sank even deeper into my lap, his limbs going limp, my own legs unable to distinguish his flesh from mine. But the burning baby slid out of me. I didn't have to fight it anymore. And I knew I would join the others, because they were my family, my people.

I said, "Listen, Nazarene, lie here as long as you want. It's too late for me to do anything else. I want to tell you, though, that if I die and hear you calling me, I will wrap the grave clothes tighter around me and stop my ears because I won't come out of the earth with worms on my cheeks. I'll wait for the real death."

He smiled like a child in its sleep.

"I'll only disturb you in this life, Martha," he said.

Legend of the Locust Root

Legend of the Locust Root

I like the legend in which Jesus rips out a locust tree root that has been ruining an old man's garden and tells the root to take wing and fly home, and it does.

The lightness of the escaping root captivates me. So many of the stories of Jesus have a heavy quality: the fishermen have worked all night and taken nothing, so Jesus tells them to drop their nets one more time, and they immediately haul up so many fish that the nets start to break. Simon becomes a disciple at once, and Jesus tells him that now he will catch human beings as he once caught fish. It makes a nice simile. A solid, serviceable, impressive miracle. But heavy, like work shoes after a muddy field.

And likewise his medical accomplishments: the lepers restored to health, the blind given back their vision. He made himself into everyone's fantasy of a truly competent doctor who never takes vacations. So what do we have today? Cataracts? Rub them with spittle. Scabies? Believe on me.

He recognized the problem himself: When Martha wanted help in the kitchen, Jesus told her that her sister Mary, who wanted to skip the housework and get to the spiritual essence, had chosen the better part. You could tell he admired Mary. Martha was too much like him: What can I do for you? Loaves and fishes for five thousand? A little something to mitigate the fear of death?

Other founders and heroes rout giants and part the Red Sea. Easy to understand the early Christians who preferred to pray to Sebastian pierced with arrows or Catherine impaled on a spiked wheel. You sympathize with their antipathy for a parable that tells you not only to carry the Roman soldier's bags but to insist on carrying them a second mile as well.

Therefore I love a legend like the locust root. He reaches his hand right through the crumbly soil and like magic pulls out a brown, hairy length of wood— this homely object that is wreaking havoc in the garden of an old man with a trick knee who hand picks bugs off his fava beans. Jesus just rips out the devil root and casts it away.

But in this legend, the devil isn't destroyed; the root doesn't end up in the trash heap. No, Jesus goes the extra mile in this legend and gives the people what they want as well as what they need.

"And the root sprouts wings and does fly."

Just lifts off on wings of bark and resin, wings that last precisely as long as it takes to fly the root to its new home. Where it drops a long way down, burrows into a thin, treeless soil, and at once its eager progeny sprout. And someone in that rocky place gives thanks for the hardy tree, and the old man gives thanks it is gone. And everyone – believer, unbeliever, disbeliever – swells with the grace of gratitude.

The Adventure of Dunzyad, Scheherezade, and the King

The Adventure of Dunzyad, Scheherezade, and the King

We used to act out stories under the orange trees in the garden. We girls played all the parts: princes, soldiers, and princesses. We weren't supposed to see boys or men, or even girls old enough to get married. The Grand Vizier visited us, though. He was in charge of the girls, and everyone had to cover their faces when he came– except for my sister Scheherezade and me, because he was our father, and our mother was his only wife.

There were a lot of things we girls weren't supposed to do or know, but we knew and we did. We would creep along the bushes and listen to our mothers whispering in the shade of the gallery. We would sneak into other parts of the palace and climb the vines and throw things over the wall at the boys.

Except for Scheherezade. She always sat reading books. She was also good at telling stories. She is a little fat, but she has a voice that makes you want to listen. The mothers used to say "How unfortunate Scheherezade was not a boy! She could study the law or follow in the footsteps of the Grand Vizier!" They also used to say how well-behaved she was, until they realized she was reading forbidden books. Then they scolded her and predicted she would turn out to be a Bad Woman. But Scheherezade just watched their mouths moving and went back to reading. Nobody tells Scheherezade what to do.

Whenever it got hot and we decided to rest, we would go into the arbor and listen to her stories. All the mothers and amahs and slaves and even the boys on the other side of the wall would lean close to listen. She told stories in which girls were the heroes and saved the kingdom, and she told stories from the old books collected by merchants and travelers through all of Persia and India and the spice-scented lands of Arabia. After we listened to her stories, we vowed that we would travel one day and see the sights for ourselves. We were going to have adventures! We were going to save the kingdom!

A girl named Fatyma, who already had breasts and shouldn't have been in our garden at all, told us we were ignorant. "Soon," said Big Mouth Fatyma, "you will all be married, and the only adventures you'll have will be in gardens a lot smaller than this one!"

"Tell her it isn't so, Scheherezade!" I cried. "Tell her we will have adventures and do great deeds!"

"We have to be ready, Dunzyad," said Scheherezade. "You never know when an adventure will start."

So we went back to playing at being bold princes and fearless soldiers and sailors.

Then one day we overhead our mothers whispering about the Great Trouble. At first, it was like a new story to us, a little less interesting than the ones with bandits and demons. This story was about how the wife of the Great King (may-God-always-bless-him!) had cheated on him. He was so furious that he began to punish the women of the kingdom.

First he killed his bad wife and all her bad hand maidens. Then he killed some bad women who had no husbands but kept big houses where they entertained men and danced and sang. Sometimes he would marry one of these rich bad women at night and kill her in the morning.

Fatyma said that the Great King (may-God-always-bless-him!) was making it impossible for a girl to have a wedding. How could you celebrate your wedding with the Grand General's son when there was a funeral every day?

46

We said, "Who cares? Who cares about funerals or weddings?"

Then Fatyma told us the King was killing other kinds of women as well. We refused to believe it until one of the mothers got a message and began shrieking and ripping her clothes and crying that her own sister had been called to marry the King.

The next morning, three girls were missing from our garden. We thought at first that they had been married to the king, but then we found out that their parents had taken them away. Everyone began to toss strange looks at our mother and even at Scheherezade and me because our father, the Grand Vizier with the jeweled scimitar, was the one in charge of bringing women to the king.

Scheherezade and I talked about it in bed that night. "So what?" I said. "It's good for the kingdom to get rid of the Bad Women. Right?"

Scheherezade said, "He isn't looking for Bad Women anymore. He's just killing."

I said, "If the Great King kills them, then they must be bad! They have to be!" When Scheherezade didn't say anything, I whispered, "Tell me a story so I can go to sleep."

She told me about a brave girl who went to the world of demons to save her father. It put me to sleep, but I had a nightmare with a demon chasing me. And the demon turned into our father, and instead of jewels on the hilt of his sword were the faces of girls I knew!

The next night, Scheherezade said, "The King must be stopped."

"Shh!" I cried. "What if he can hear through walls?"

Scheherezade said, "I know a story about a man who was sick in the brain."

And instead of asking her to tell the story, I said, "Did he get better?"

"Yes," said Scheherezade, "after much sacrifice and courage on the part of a princess."

Meanwhile, the mothers were saying that there would be no more young women in the whole kingdom. One mother came to the garden and told us her daughter had died of fever in the night, but we knew, by the expression on her face, that she was lying. The girl had left the city or was hiding in a cellar or in a leather bottle like the forty thieves in the story. I envied the girls who were somewhere else and not seeing the sad garden with no one in it and fruit falling from the trees.

I said to Scheherezade, "I want to hide too."

Scheherezade said, "I want to cure the King."

I said, "Let's run away like the others."

The next day, no one came to the garden except us and Fatyma. And the day after that, our father came. We hadn't seen him in weeks. He was dressed as beautifully as ever, with all the jewels encrusting the hilt of his sword, but his face was long and wrinkled, and his step uncertain. When he came close, we could see shudders running through his shoulders.

Our mother called for sherbet and fans, but he refused everything. He sat in the arbor. When our mother tried to speak, he waved his hand to silence her. Finally, he shouted that he wanted to speak to the mother of Fatyma. Fatyma's mother started to scream. He shouted again, and this time Fatyma's mother came, rending her garments and making her throat vibrate with that sound called ululation.

"It is a great honor," said the Grand Vizier, "to marry the Great King."

"No!" screamed Fatyma's mother. "No!"

Fatyma pressed herself against the wall, not moving.

"The King has asked for the virgin daughter of one of the great families– "

"She is engaged to be married!" cried Fatyma's mother.

Our father bent his head and shaded his eyes. "The engagement has been broken. She is to go to the King tonight."

Now Fatyma started to wail too.

"Your husband sent me to tell you to prepare her for her wedding with– the Great– King (may-God-always...)" And that was as far as he got before he covered his whole face with his hands.

So Fatyma was crying, and her mother was hitting her fists on her chest, and our mother was on her knees praying, and all the slaves and servants were wailing and waving their arms and ululating. It was a terrible din!

Scheherezade stepped forward and stood in front of our father. "O Great Grand Vizier," she said, and they fell silent to listen to her. "O Great Grand Vizier," she said, "My mother's husband, father of my sister, and father of me! Hear O Father!"

He raised a sleeve to cover his face. Scheherezade reached out to kiss his hand, but he jerked it away. "Not that hand!" he said.

"It wasn't you, who killed the girls, O Father," she said. "It was the Great, Dread, May-God-bless-his heart King. He is the one who is sick!" Everyone gasped, but they gasped even more when she said, "I will go to the King instead of Fatyma." Her voice carried through the whole courtyard.

"Quiet!" cried the Grand Vizier. "You are an ignorant little girl."

"An ignorant little girl, Scheherezade!" said our mother.

"Let her go!" cried Fatyma.

"I will go to the King," said Scheherezade.

The Grand Vizier's lips began to twitch, and I thought he would strike her across the face, but instead, he said, "Let me tell you a story."

He told a story about animals who could talk and got in trouble by being too clever. Then he told a story about a man who understood the animals but didn't understand women and had to learn to beat his wife. Scheherezade's stories were better.

When story was over, she said, "I will go to the King tonight."

He told more stories about punishment and death. When he stopped talking, Scheherezade said again that she was going to the king, and he shouted, "No you aren't, Fatyma goes tonight!"

And all the noise started up again. The Grand Vizier wrapped himself in his robes and departed, but he left soldiers to make sure Fatyma didn't run away, and soon her own father came with red eyes to prepare her.

Scheherezade pulled me over into the galleries where the women usually sat. "Tonight I am going tonight to save the Kingdom."

"You don't have to, Scheherezade," I said. "Our father will protect us."

She waved me silent, just as our father had waved our mother silent. "I am going to the King, but I need your help." All I had to do, she told me, was come with her and wait till she looked at me and nodded two times. Then I was to shout as loud as I could: "Oh let us hear one of my sister Scheherezade's stories!" Her idea was that she would tell the King such good stories that he would never want to kill anyone again.

I said, "Let's run away. Let's hide in the cellars."

"This is our adventure, Dunzyad," she said. "If you want an adventure, you have to take the one they give you."

So while everyone else cried and howled and dressed Fatyma in her best clothes, Scheherezade and I slipped out of the Girls' Garden into the long halls of the King's Great Palace. It was already dusk, so it was easy to hide behind a screen or in a staircase. But the halls seemed empty. So many people had run away that we stopped hiding and walked boldly down the corridors as if we were just two servant girls on an errand.

I thought: Someday, someone will tell the Adventure of Dunzyad and Scheherezade.

We knew we were near the King's chambers when we saw Mamelukes in the hall. Mamelukes are the tallest men in the kingdom, special soldier-slaves brought from around the world, even from the cold countries where people have no color in their skin or eyes.

Scheherezade shouted at the top of her lungs, "Make way! Make way for the daughters of the Grand Vizier! We are going to the King tonight!"

We passed through hall after hall, shouting at the Mamelukes: "Make way! Make way! We are going to the King tonight!" At last we came to a great arched door guarded by the two biggest Mamelukes of all: one was as colorless as ice from the North, the other glowing black like onyx from the South.

Scheherezade shouted, "Step aside, Mamelukes! We are going to the King tonight."

At that moment there was shouting from inside and we were almost knocked over by a crowd of servants with big platters of food, all spilled and broken. Inside, the shouts turned to groans, and I grabbed her arm.

She said, "It is better to have an adventure than sit and wait."

All I had to do, I reminded myself, was wait til she gave me the nod and shout Oh sister Scheherezade, tell us a story.

We stepped into a high, dark room with a wide low table covered by more spilled food and broken plates and bottles. It smelled bad in there, of rotten food and not enough cleaning.

I think the man in the bed needed cleaning too.

It was the King, and once I saw him, I didn't notice anything else for a long time.

He was lying on his side in bed as if he wanted to be asleep instead of awake. Only his face and one arm were out of the covers, and everything about him seemed thick and swollen. His nose was huge and his lips pouched out, and one eye was squinted and one was wide and staring. His hair stood up in all directions.

The huge head lifted up when he noticed us and turned from side to side like a big puppet. "What? What?" he said, and raised himself higher. "It's a little girl," he said. "It's two little girls."

"We're the daughters of the Grand Vizier," said Scheherezade. "I'm here instead of Fatyma."

"Who?"

"Fatyma. She's the girl who was supposed to come tonight."

"Girl?" said the King. "No girls! I only— eat— women!" And he reached out a huge hand all covered with ruby rings and swept more dishes and food off the table, crashed them onto the floor. "Go away!" he shouted. "Where's my dinner?"

The servants came running back. "You sent your food away O Great King (may-God-always-bless-you!)!"

The King was rising up out of his covers, his naked chest dark and hairy and his huge face twisted with anger. He was growing larger and larger.

Fear began to close in on me like the darkness. I was sure I was about to die or faint, so without waiting for the signal, I screamed, "Oh listen to my sister Scheherezade! She came to tell a wonderful story! Listen to her story!"

The next thing I knew, I was curled up on the floor half under the table with my face next to a smashed banana. The servants were gone again, and Scheherezade was sitting on the side of the King's bed telling a story about a demon who was going to kill a man for spitting olive pits.

I must have missed the beginning, but there were definitely olive pits in the story, and also on the floor with me and the banana.

Scheherezade sat with her hands folded neatly in her lap, and every once in a while the King grunted. The story went on and on, and like magic the night passed and dawn caught us. "That's all," said Scheherezade.

"Finish it," said the King.

"I can finish it tonight." she said.

I called out, "After she finishes that one, she'll tell you another one better than the first!"

The King sighed. "Come back tonight then. I think I'm going to work today. I haven't worked in a long time. Go away, little girl, and take your little sister Shadow too. But come back tonight or I shall be very angry."

He almost sounded like he was joking. He almost sounded like a regular person. He had made up a nickname for me the way our father used to do. So we stepped through the great doors and discovered that the hall outside was full of people: Our Father was there with his garments torn and our mother with her face exposed. More Mamelukes than I ever guessed existed, and Fatyma's entire family dressed in their best clothing, and servants asleep on the floor.

From inside the King shouted for food, for his bath, he had to go to work! He wanted the Grand Vizier!

"Are you alive?" our father said. "Both of you?"

Scheherezade was so tired she just nodded.

I said, "She has to come back tonight to finish the story."

All the people sighed. The Grand Vizier said, "Was it the story of the merchant who hit his wife with sticks?"

Scheherezade shook her head and ran to our mother who lifted her up in her arms. She said, "I'll tell that one another day, Father."

Scheherezade and I slept for hours and hours and woke up and ate olives and bread and fruit and took baths and looked at the toys and new dresses sent by the Great King (may-God-always-bless-him!). He sent a message, too, that he felt better than he had in a year. He wanted Scheherezade to come back. He wanted more stories. He wanted stories tonight and every night. And Little Sister Shadow should come too.

Scheherezade frowned. "I didn't think we would have to go every night."

"Do you suppose we'll ever get to play in the garden again?"

She shrugged. "I don't know. In the stories, you know what's coming next. In real life, it's a mystery."

That isn't the end of this story. First came the hundreds of tales Scheherezade and Dunzyad. told the King. Some nights he would fall asleep early, and sometimes he was in a dark mood and didn't like the stories and threatened to kill us, but he never did.

Then Scheherezade became a woman, and after her, I became a woman, and we continued to go to the King every night, and time passed, and she and I both had sons and daughters for the king. And for many years the King was calm, and the country was happy. He named Scheherezade's oldest son to be his heir and the people loved the boy, and they loved the King too.

But then, many years later, the King's sickness returned, and he began to storm and threaten again, and sometimes he killed servants and strangers. Then he began to say he would kill his children because they were plotting to steal his Kingdom.

And one night, after Scheherezade had told the King the story about a man who has dreams and dreams within dreams, he fell asleep. I was napping on the couch, and like a dream within my dream, something happened in the night.

It seemed that the magic knife from the story appeared, and struck, and saved the kingdom.

In the morning, Scheherezade and I screamed for the Mamelukes because evil jinn had visited in the night and cut the king's throat. The Mamelukes agreed that it could only have been the jinn, and our father the old Grand Vizier agreed it could only have been the jinn, and he declared a year of mourning for the King.

So Scheherezade's son became the new King (may-his-name-be-blessed), and when our father died, my oldest son became the Grand Vizier. This brought to our kingdom a time of great peace, and we found kind, scholarly men to be the husbands of our daughters, and we taught all our children to be slow to anger and faithful to one another, and because our children are faithful, the people of the kingdom are faithful, and we shall all live happily until we die.

Her Statue

Her Statue

There was once a village where the primary industry was carving in wood. Traditionally, the only proper subject was the figure of a man with an exaggerated and highly decorated phallus, but one day a young girl began looking at her reflection in the pool from which they drew their water. The other women finished filling their jugs and went to hoe, but she was still gazing and wondering: "Why don't they carve women's figures? Why don't they make me?"

She went to the headman, who was an uncle of her mother's, and said, "Listen, Wisdom, why is it taboo to make images of women's bodies? I looked in the water, and my body is beautiful."

The old headman might have told her that this style of carving had been done in their village since time immemorial, or he might have tried to convince her that only the straightest lines have beauty, or he might have reminded her that the warrior tribe to the east required this particular style of statue in tribute, but he was a man of action. He quickly arranged her marriage to the best young artisan in the village, a boy whose body became almost as beautiful in her eyes as her own.

After their first child was born, she came to the old headman again, not noticing that he was dying. "Listen, Wisdom, you were right. Since you gave me a husband, I have learned and considered. What I saw in the water was unfinished. Now I have dreamed a dream, I have a vision for the artists. They must take the largest tree trunk in the forest and carve three figures around its circumference. First will be a young girl full of questions; then one pregnant with her eyes turned inward; finally, a woman with full breasts– the mother!"

But the old headman himself had begun to look only inward. "Come back tomorrow," he murmured, but when she returned, he had gone to the place from which nothing is ever revealed.

Her husband was elected headman in his place.

For the glory of the ancestors and the village, and to placate the restless tribes in the East, the new headman undertook to carve the largest tree trunk in the forest. Twenty strong men were needed to drag the sacred bole to a special stockade near his house.

"Listen," said the woman to her husband. "I have had a vision to inform your great work. It involves roundness. It involves the figures of women."

Now the new headman admired and loved his wife, and he allowed that her idea was possible, but he added, "Of course, it is not permitted for women to invent."

"Of course," she said. "And this was not an invention, but a gift in a dream from the ancestors."

The work went slowly, but the woman's husband was an excellent artist, and bit by bit, with great effort, and after many observations of gourds and melons and baby's backsides and other round things, the statue began to take on a tentative form like nothing else ever made in that village.

When it was nearly finished, a delegation of elders had to come and approve. The woman served them a feast, then she laid out newly woven mats on the ground so their walk to the carving yard would be clean and sweet scented. She listened at the gate, and there was silence for a long time.

When they came out, they gathered the hems of their ceremonial robes about them to avoid her touch, and they took her husband with them for a long purification ritual. When he came back, he was not allowed to see her, although she was permitted to make his meals and empty his slop bucket.

They guarded the gate so she could not go in, and she could hear him inside hacking at their great work, hour after hour, and when the enclosure was finally opened, she saw that he had hacked away the fullness and fastened on a phallus with pegs and glue.

She should have guessed what he was doing, of course, but something overtook her, and she went insane: "Aiiy! Aiiy! Aiiy!" she cried, and people came running from all over the village to see what would happen. "Aiiy Aiiy Aiiy! Traitor! Coward!"

"I am a carver," he said severely, "and I carve what a carver carves, which is only the Great Lingam!"

She howled and threw glue and shavings of wood at him.

He shouted, "You bewitched me!"

She chased him through the village threatening him with his carving tools. "I'll carve my own!" she screamed. "I'll carve the likeness of a woman on a stick and beat you to death! I'll carve women on funeral faggots and burn the whole village!"

These threats caused the old men to gather again to take action, but she didn't wait. She ran off to the forest, where no one goes alone, leaving her children to beg at the neighbor's, leaving her husband to be deposed from office for lack of dignity, leaving the statue to be floated down the river to the warrior tribe with its phallus aimed at the sky.

In the forest, she found a fallen tree that was even larger than her husband's. She made a fire to keep the snakes away, and she slipped back into the village and stole tools and took her little daughter but left her son. She made a lean-to for herself and her daughter and began to carve the tree trunk.

She had never been allowed to hold the tools; she was untrained in the methods and the art. Six times an hour her chisel slipped and she howled in frustration. Her daughter helped a little, but mostly she picked fruit and dug roots and killed living things to roast in the coals. On the second day the woman chopped off the end of her finger, and on the third day, she chopped off her statue's nose. In her determination to finish the torso, she sometimes worked in the dark, lightheaded with hunger, and one time she chiseled away its left breast.

After a few days, her daughter went back to the village.

Days passed, weeks, and months. Since she knew that only the insane live in the forest, she understood that she must be insane, or else go back to the village too.

So she sawed the still unfinished statue into sections and dragged the smallest one with her back to the village. She started to live in the small storage hut behind her house. Her children came out to sit with her, and her husband knew she was there. Every day she went back to the forest and brought one of the chunks of her statue, and when they were all in the hut, she began to cook for her husband again.

She still slept in the hut, but she cooked, and swept out the yard, and her children sometimes slept in the hut with her.

After about a year, people got used to having her back. Her husband was given work again, but he had been replaced as headman. One night, when the men were drinking fermented fruit juice, she had her daughter and sons help her drag out the pieces of her statue to the front of her house. She stood the sections one on top of the other until the whole statue was there for the world to see.

The men all slept that night in the drinking lodge, but in the morning, the villagers came out and saw her monstrous statue in front of her house. Her husband didn't know whether to attack or flee. The new headman, however, was wiser though not as good a carver as her husband.

He told all the people to gather and see what the hen who wanted to be a rooster had made. The people gathered around the pile of tree chunks with the lopsided mouth and single breast. The new headman started to laugh, and the people laughed. They laughed until the urine ran down their legs.

Her disgraced husband laughed the loudest. "Look, look," he said. "Just what you'd expect! It isn't a woman, it isn't a man! The crowing hen carved a capon!"

The woman sat cross legged beside her statue and listened to them laugh. She sat by her statue all day, and slept there that night. People threw vegetable skins sometimes, and once or twice a drunken man pissed on it. But after a week, people began to go about their business. No one paid any attention to her statue.

She stopped sleeping outside to guard it, and one of the neighbors gave her seed to get her garden started again. The head man assigned her husband to work on a big project with some other men. She started sleeping in the house again, and before long, she was pregnant and living like the other people, although they still sometimes talked about her with a kind of amazement.

They lived quietly and had altogether five children, and the children grew up climbing the big statue and the boys became carvers like their father, and one eventually became a head man. Her daughter married out of the village and moved away, and it was said that in the village to the west where she lived, the women made small exquisite carvings from fallen nuts that brought great wealth to their families.

When the woman's husband was old, at one festival season, he drank too much and died.

After he was dead, the woman sometimes worked on the statue again, trying to make it round. She was the only woman in that village permitted to use the tools, and for this reason, young people sometimes came to ask her advice.

"I used to have hair," she would tell them. "I used to be the wife of a headman but he was pulled down because I went crazy. I lived in the forest alone for five months. I had five children, and one of them is your headman now. They say my daughter carves in that place where she lives. But I don't take credit for that. The only thing of my own is my statue.

"So here is my best advice: do what the others do, and don't ask questions. Your life will be like a long sleep. Or, go crazy and live alone, and you will be miserable. Live to be old and miserable or old and respected; your organs will shrivel up either way.

"But I'll tell you this: no one will ever make a thing as big and ugly as my statue."

The Great Wolf

The Great Wolf

He was weaving a basket, and she reclined against a bank of ferns with her fingers knit under her belly. At the edge of the woods the lame roebuck had been cornered, and was giving itself to the wolf pack. The roebuck did not die at once but lay awhile with its head up and eyes wide as the pack began pulling out its entrails.

She said, "Do you suppose one day we'll have to look a wolf in the eye and say, 'Take me?'"

He shrugged. "I don't know. Maybe, if we get weak." Lately he had been full of his own strength; he had broken their records for distance swimming and highest tree climbed.

She thought she knew the reason for all his efforts to prove himself.

She said, "We can ask Our Mother when She comes."

He jerked at a reed. "Are you going to start that again?"

"What else could She be but a mother? She who brought forth everything."

"A father," he said. The argument had been going on for many seasons, playfully at first, but with more urgency now that she appeared to be pregnant. "Our Father," he said firmly. "He displays the sky and the land before us as the peacock displays his feathers. He plants his seed throughout the earth."

"The male has nothing to do with it," she said. "The male is for decoration." She didn't really believe that; the One would never waste so many creatures, but it always got a gratifying reaction from him. For several seconds he tried to keep weaving, then he threw the basket aside and exploded down the slope at top speed.

"You aren't pregnant anyhow!" he shouted. "You ate too many yams!" He leaped over the carcass of the roebuck, scattering the wolves, and disappeared into the forest.

Poor thing, she thought. He has no idea what it feels like to be full of creation. Of course the One was a Mother.

She took a nap, and after stretching awake, walked up the hill with the One Tree on it. She pulled some grain and chewed it as she went up. When he came out of his pout, they wold milk the goats together. She sat on the fence that enclosed the One Tree in a roundish yard. It was a low rock tumble, the only purposeful stone structure they had ever seen except for things they had built themselves—their swimming dam, their arrangements of rocks for grinding nuts and grain. The wall had always fascinated them, and they had asked the One which animal built it, but the One had directed their attention from the wall to the tree and told them not to eat the fruit, which was no problem, because the tree never bore any.

The big serpent was in the enclosure near the tree. She had never liked him very much; he tended to talk a lot. She was about to swing her legs back over the wall and leave, but she saw he was holding an apple in his jaws. That startled her, and she glanced at the One Tree, which was laden with more apples than she had ever seen on any tree before. Many had fallen to the ground, and there were piles of nearly perfect ones on top of a rotten brown mash. The big serpent made no effort to swallow his apple. He rested his head on a flat boulder, most of his voluminous body hidden in the grass.

She said, "You got that apple from the One Tree."

He brought his eyelids together in what she took to be assent.

"You aren't supposed to eat apples from the One Tree."

He unhinged his jaws and eased his throat around the apple so that it slid out of sight, stretching his throat into an apple shape. Hoarsely he said, "Why not?" and regurgitated the apple.

"You don't even eat apples," she said. "Snakes don't eat apples."

The serpent let the apple roll off his tongue, across the flat boulder, stopping just at the edge. "I've had so many," he said. "I can't even get one more down."

"You haven't eaten any. The One forbids it."

He lifted his head. Mock surprise, she thought. "Really? The One forbade you? Just you, or both of you?"

"No one is allowed," she said, feeling uneasy because there had been no one around except the two of them when the One said it.

"Wrong," said the serpent, drowsily lowering his head. Gray head, flat as the rock, pinkish rhomboid scales shimmering when the light hit them, fading into the shadows at his sides. "Peculiar, though," said the serpent, "that the One gave you two special instructions."

She sat on the grass and put her elbows on his boulder and looked him in the eye. The apple he had slavered on was between them, and she knocked it off the rock. "We're special," she said. "Everyone knows that. We're smart, we make things, and we talk."

"Everyone talks."

"No, they don't. Not anymore. No one talks but us and you. We got smarter and they got stupider."

The serpent said, "They still talk. You just can't understand them."

This had not occurred to her. She glanced down the hill, hoping he would turn up to help her dispute with the serpent. No sign of him, but a lot of clouds were gathering, and the wind seemed unseasonably chilly up on this hill. The sun fell in a broad warm band by the stream where the deer and goats grazed, but here it was gray and chilly.

"Have an apple," said the serpent. "Then you won't be so stupid anymore."

"I'd eat one if it made you shut up."

"That's as good a reason as any," said the serpent. He stirred, the whole length of him rustling far out in the grass. He was moving slowly these days, she thought. Maybe the time had come for him to give himself to an eagle, or the maggots. Everything up here seemed old. The One Tree was the oldest living thing they knew; it was wrenched, twisted, and huge in girth. She wished the apples would break its branches off. It was time for the tree to give itself, too.

She said, "The One never forbad apples off the ground, of course."

"Hah," said the serpent.

Actually, it was vague in her mind, the wording. The One did not precisely use words anyhow. Or else she had forgotten them. A lot of things seemed vague to her just now. The smell of fermenting apple juice clouded her mind. She knew they used to be able to talk to the animals, and she thought maybe they had once been able to talk to the plants, too, and perhaps to the stones and wind. She had a moment, she saw down a corridor with great curtained walls, no top or bottom, a narrowing like sheets of lightning and the aurora borealis: high and brilliant folds. Far down this corridor were things they had lost, beyond reach, infinitely far.

"Look at you," said the serpent. "Who are you trying to fool? You're going to eat an apple. That's the only thing special about you and him. Nobody else would dare. The One knows you're going to do it. The One knows everything, you might as well go ahead. You really don't have any choice."

"No choice!" she was indignant and embraced her indignation because it was more familiar than those corridors of loss. She scooped up the apple the serpent had mouthed and tossed it at him. He dodged. "I have lots of choices. I can pelt you with apples, for instance." She threw more apples at him till he moved off, and then she sat, dead center, on the rock with her legs folded. She sat there for several seconds watching the serpent coil and uncoil, trying to get himself comfortable again. Then she spotted a single perfect rosy apple within easy reach on top of a pile of rotting ones. She leaned over awkwardly to pick it up, then polished it with a section of her hair and then between her breasts. Tossed it from hand to hand, enjoying the serpent's side-to-side motion as he followed the juggling. "You see, I have lots of choices. I can pelt you, I can play with this one. I can do anything I want." She was gratified to feel the truth of this. She could do what she wanted. She was hungry, but she didn't feel like eating this particular apple. "And even if I did eat it, it would be because I just happened to feel hungry."

"The reason is immaterial," said the serpent.

She licked the apple. Ran her tongue all over it, just to show the serpent. Or herself, or someone. The One used to tell them to avoid all kinds of things: mushrooms, bark, the rapids in the river. Rules to keep them from harm. The One Tree was the same kind of thing, no doubt. Something they would eventually understand. "I can do anything I want," she said. "No one can stop me."

The serpent closed his eyes and didn't open them, as if he'd gotten bored with the conversation.

So she ate the apple slowly. It was bland. Perhaps the One Tree in this late fruition had overextended itself, or else the ones still on the branches were better, but she drew the line at that. I don't choose to pick and eat, she thought. I only choose to eat this one fallen apple. She sat awhile, burped, picked some peel out of her teeth, and tossed the core at the serpent to wake him. "Well, I ate it."

"You'll be sorry," said the serpent.

"I won't." She threw another apple at him, and he didn't move. Let it bounce off his hide.

"That's the beginning," he said.

"I've been throwing things at you for years. You deserve it."

He seemed to stretch his mouth into a smile. "The beginning of your knowledge."

She was half inclined to believe him. Was she seeing more sharply? She had a slight headache, as if she had been concentrating too hard. Quite a high wind up here now, and the continuing strangeness of shadow while the woods and valley basked in sun. "What knowledge? Are you my teacher?"

The serpent coiled his hindmost parts in a great spiral of rising folds and lifted his front in a show of head swaying and tongue flickering. "This knowledge," he said softly, repeating himself in a hiss: "This knowledge. Look at me."

She shuddered, and the serpent sensed it with his trembling tongue. His eyes fixed on her: tiny pricks of cold light, and she thought she knew what the mice must feel when they come tripping down their little paths and the serpent blocks their way.

"I have a Great Wolf," she said. "Just like everyone else, I have a Great Wolf." She shook her head. She was not a mouse. "But I'm not giving myself. I am strong and healthy, and I am not ready to give myself."

She touched the serpent's head hanging before her in the air, touched the flat of it with her fingertips and began to stroke. He closed his eyes A sigh seemed to run through his coils, and he sank gradually down onto the stone. She rubbed his head over and over, began to massage his thick body. "What will the One do when it is known that I ate the apple?" The snake opened an eye for an instant, and she had the chill again, the paralyzing speck of pupil in the vortex of the glitter. That was the snake's answer, and then he gave himself over to her massage. She pressed hard, working her way down his neck, behind his jaws. She used both hands on his supple, long muscles. She made a collar of her hands around his neck. "But who will tell the One?" She tightened her grip, beyond massage, and the snake's eyes popped open. "Who knows I ate the apple?"

He began to thrash, his eyes yellow and flat now, no longer bearing any messages, all energy in the torque through his vast length. She tightened her grip till his tongue came out and he gave unvoiced hisses, but she couldn't throttle him to silence, he was too strong. She grunted and strained, and tears of anger came to her eyes. "Give yourself to me, snake," she cried. She tried to use him like a lash and break his neck, but his body was too heavy, and he redirected his coils, trying to encircle her. She sidestepped, pushed his head down on the flat bolder with one hand and seized a stone with the other, began to pound the head, dancing side to side all the time to avoid his grasp. He bled over one eye and thrashed less. She was getting tired too. Everything seemed to slow, and she had the sensation of being watched, feared it was the One, and whirled around.

He was sitting on the wall with his arms crossed. "What are you doing to the serpent?"

She dropped the stone. Her hair was in her eyes: she was in a greasy sweat. The wind was taking away the moisture, cooling her too quickly. "The snake was about to give himself to me."

"To eat?"

"I had a hunger for animal flesh."

"For snake? We don't eat snake. And he wasn't giving himself to you anyhow. He was fighting."

"He was going to give himself soon." She kept looking at his face, and she saw he was waiting for the rest of it, for the real reason. They always told each other the real thing, otherwise, why were there two of them? So she said, "I suppose it was less of a yen for snake meat— and more for apples."

His eyes widened. "You ate from the One Tree?"

"I took one off the ground."

"You really did it, you really ate from the One Tree?" He was amazed, he started walking in front of her, paced to the tree, paced back. The snake moved too, blinked, slipped his head off the rock and slithered away, saying nothing, and with no part lifted off the ground.

"It was a mistake," she said. "I shouldn't have done it."

"What happened after you ate it?"

"I found out the answer to the question. I found out that there is a Great Wolf, and one day I have to give myself just as the roebuck gave himself."

"What else?"

"Nothing else. I tried to take the snake's life so it wouldn't tell the One."

He stopped in front of her. "There must have been more." He tapped her on the shoulder, to make her look at him. She was finding it hard to pay attention; she could see the shape of the sun through the clouds, and the sun was yellow like the eye of the Great Wolf. The young thing growing inside her seemed to be rising up, pressing against her lungs from below, and the wind was stealing her breath at the same time.

He turned his tap into a little shove. "Tell me, or I'm going to eat one myself. You're not the only one who can do things."

She looked at him, how he was taller than he was, and had more muscle-mass in his shoulders. "Don't, please."

"I'm taking mine off the tree," he said, and like a leaping fish arced into the air and snatched an apple and almost before his feet were on the ground again bit into it, glaring at her, chomping and snorting. "Look at me eating!" he shouted. "Look at me eat! You think you know so much because of that— " he pointed at her belly. "Look at me!" He shook branches, he took a bite out of an apple and threw it away; he took bites of apples still on the tree. He broke branches, he stripped the bark. "When does it come?" he asked. "When do you know? What didn't you tell me?"

"I'm going down," she said. "This is a bad place."

He shoved her back onto the rock. "You aren't going anywhere till you tell me the rest of it." He walked in front of her. He took bites of more apples and tossed them away. "I'll tell you what I want to know. I want you to tell me that what you have in your stomach is mine. I made it. Tell me that when it comes out, I can have it."

"The Great Wolf will come too soon."

He raised a fist. "Say it. Not that it matters, because when it comes out, I can take it from you. I can take anything from you because I'm stronger."

"Are you going to take me? Are you the Great Wolf?"

He sat down on the rock with his back to her. He was silent for a long time, then he rubbed his eyes and shook his head. "That tree makes poison apples," he said. "I think we should go somewhere and recover. You're shivering. I'm going to build you a warm place to rest till that comes out. I'll take care of you."

She shrugged. She thought: I am the weak deer that will soon be taken.

He was sharpening sticks and building a protective palisade around their new dwelling when the One came. The One, faceless out of the whirlwind, said, What is this? Why didn't you come when I called?

He answered hastily, "Oh we didn't hear you. We've been inside pounding and building."

She came out and said, "Listen, I'm ready. Show me your yellow eyes and your jaws. I can't stand waiting."

"Shut up," he whispered. He was frantic; he tried to cover her mouth, but she was stronger than she'd been pretending, and she pushed him away.

"We ate the apples," she said. "We know you, Great Wolf. Take us now."

The One said, You have decided that you know me? You tell me when to take you? I'll take you when I'm ready, little foolish one. You have long to live and much to endure. Now, get out of that pile of dry sticks.

There was lightning; there was a wind. Their hut began to crackle with flames.

The one said, Get away from those sticks and get out of my garden.

Their shelter blew apart, and twigs and crisps of burning leaf flew around their legs, stung them and herded them away. They ran, she heavy and angry because nothing was settled after all; he, trying to protect her from the One's wrath.

She avoided him, and turned back toward the flaming swords crossed against their return. "You mean we're to know it's coming, but not when?"

But when the One spoke, they no longer understood.

Baucis and Philemon # 3

Baucis and Philemon # 3

....and as the tops of the trees grew over their two faces, they exchanged words, while they still could, saying, in the same breath: "Farewell, O dear companion," as, in the same breath, the bark covered them, concealing their mouths.
– Ovid's Metamorphosis Book VIII, lines 679-724 (A.S. Kline version)

And Baucis hastily cried out,
"My dear, I see your forehead sprout!"
– "Baucis and Philemon" by Jonathan Swift

W hen I came out after my run in the park, the woman was sitting on the bench where I usually stretch. I immediately categorized her as old and possibly homeless, although her knit cap and matching scarf looked new. She had several fat plastic shopping bags at her feet, and she was shuffling through an enormous leather pocketbook.

I said, "Do you mind if I use this end to stretch?"

"No, of course not," she said.

I hiked up my left foot onto the bench and leaned over, started working on my tendons.

She said, "I was wondering, did you happen to see my husband? He's on the tall side, very lean."

I shook my head and kept stretching.

She watched me for a few seconds, then pulled a few foil wrapped objects out of the bag and lined them up on the slats beside her. The objects looked like food. She said, "He used to stay out for a couple of days at a time, but not since his bout of pneumonia."

"Sorry," I muttered, beginning to regret I'd asked to share the bench.

"He thinks he's a tree."

Then I realized I had seen her husband: a stringy individual in gray sweats standing on one leg next to a big oak tree. I had assumed it was Tai Chi. I said, "Does he have a beard?"

"He doesn't shave anymore. He looks scruffy, doesn't he? He's totally crazy."

I stopped in mid stretch, suspended over my knee.

She seemed to know she had caught my attention. She smiled, a very small smile, her little mouth surprisingly pink, as were her cheeks. She was wearing a long quilted coat, and the knit cap and scarf were pink and lavender. She was coming into sharp focus in front of me. Her face, and then her bag, which I recognized as Coach. It's not that I'm all about designer handbags, but in high school I had a job at the outlet stores. In the chocolate shop, next door to Coach, and we always had our biggest crowds during their sales.

She said, "Do you want to hear?"

"Okay," I said, giving up and sitting down. I've never liked stretching anyhow.

She was still checking what was in the bag: a thermos came out now. "Well, it starts with my family's dry cleaning shop in Queens. I always worked there, even after I started college. He never intended to. He had aspirations in other directions, in many, many directions: he wanted to be a journalist, a lawyer, a college professor. But we fell into it, you see. My family owned the building, so when I got pregnant and dropped out, it was easy to accept an apartment, and since we were there, to help out in the shop, and later, more and more, covering for my parents when they got sick. We had children. Do you understand how things just happen? You start one way, and it all goes off track."

For just a moment, I thought, like me— not taking the job I really wanted because the man I really wanted needed to stay here, but he didn't stay with me, and now I have this life

80

instead of some other one. But it's not the same at all, I thought. I've still got everything before me.

"My parents died," she said. "He insisted it was the chemicals, and how we had to get out or we were going to die early too. Maybe it was all those years of the chemicals that made him crazy. Or may just the resentment, that he didn't get what he wanted. I was okay, I had our kids, two boys, big successes, a doctor and an MBA, although we haven't seen them in three years, but that's because he's estranged. He estranged his own children."

She shook her head and seemed to be waiting for me to say something. I grunted the slightest bit. I didn't want her to think I was identifying with her.

So she went on. "Then came the thing that happened. They wanted our building, the developers. We were the last little link in their big plan to raze the neighborhood and put up luxury housing, and they offered us a truly fabulous sum to leave. Which we wanted to do anyhow, you understand, so it appeared to be a godsend. They came, they offered, we walked away with an enormous sum of money just for being indolent and not selling earlier." She pointed across the street at a beautiful prewar apartment building. "We bought our apartment cash. I wanted a place with guest rooms for the boys and their families. I was picturing holidays, family meals. I didn't expect he'd go crazy and estrange the boys, that he'd be a stranger. That's what estrangement means, you know.

"I think he started going crazy as soon as he got his heart's desire, which was freedom from the business. He had complained, he had talked about traveling, taking classes, starting over, getting a degree in philosophy. He was going to be a painter, take cruises to the Antarctic. But once there was nothing to complain about, no regular hours, he had no idea what to do with himself. Mostly he read the papers, and when he'd finished the papers, he read the newer news on the computer. He muttered and complained about the state of the world.

"I wanted a place in Florida in the winter. I went to see the boys, and this was before the estrangement, but he wouldn't go. He had a new obsession. He gave up the regular news, started studying money. He wanted to become an investor, a coupon clipper.

"And soon of course he was muttering and complaining about the market. But it all got much worse when our older boy, that's the doctor, wanted to borrow money. He wanted to buy a building, become a landlord as well as a physician, rent to other doctors. Buy a big machine of some kind. I don't know if it was a good idea or bad to do these things, but my husband exploded. He didn't say maybe or we'll think about it, he made speeches about how the boy was irresponsible, it was the wrong time for investing, he would not lend a penny, no one understands money anymore! It was terrible. And then the younger one took the part of the older one, and bam, there's a family fight, all these stubborn people, a big fight, a monumental fight, by phone, by email, face-to-face, and suddenly they're estranged. I mean, I call them when he's out of the house, I'm not estranged, but we don't see them and since the tree thing started, I'm afraid to go away even for a day.

"Things deteriorated fast. He came to a new conclusion, that the underlying problem was the monetary system corrupting our morals, or something like that. You'd think this would lead to an apology over making a big deal about lending it, but no, he's too stubborn to apologize.

"So one day he's saying it isn't just money, it is much, much more, it's all the shit— pardon my vulgarity, but that's the way he started talking— all the shit we drop, we stir up, we create. And that's when he started this project to become a tree. Do you want an apple?"

I didn't.

She unwrapped one of the foil packages, gazed at a small possibly organic McIntosh as if she wasn't sure where it had come from, then balled it back up again in foil. "For the longest time, I tired to be reasonable. 'Why trees?' I said. 'Why in the park? Mediating, yoga, I understand that. But the Buddha lived in India you know. It's warm all year round in India.' So then he decided I was part of the problem. And he'd stop speaking to me. He'd just stare like I was something unpleasant.

"Which drives me crazy I should say. I can stand just about anything but that you should ignore me. So I'd lose it a little myself. 'What about muggers?' I'd yell. 'Do you think they won't touch you because you're communing with nature? All it takes is one blow on the skull from some hooligan! What's so bad about our bed where you've slept fifty years? Explain to me, I'm not stupid, I should be able to understand. What's it all about?'

"'Stillness,' he answered.

"'Stillness!' I say. 'Stillness is for when you're dead! I want to travel or go dancing. I want the opposite of stillness!'

"'Exactly,' he says, and went to the park."

She looked at me. "I bet at your age, whatever your problems are, you think life gets easier, don't you? You think if you get married or get over the fight with your boyfriend or whatever, everything will be smooth sailing. Am I right?"

"Things are going fine for me," I said.

"When I was your age, I assumed that it would get calmer. I understood about bad health, because of my parents, but I always figured that if you live long, if you have reasonable health, you would have some kind of equanimity or equilibrium. That once the periods and hormonal nonsense are over, you'd live less like on a roller coaster. But it turns out, it's no better, it's the same except no excuses, just the raw hard thing itself. And no hope that things have to get better soon. Why should they?"

I said, "I have to go soon."

"Sure. I'm almost finished with my story. I told myself for a while that after a few nights of camping out, he would give up talking to trees and come home, but instead he only came by the apartment to get a snack and practice speeches: 'The tree grows gradually, perfectly, branches balanced by roots. Can animals comprehend the ineluctable serenity of the tree? The beauty of photosynthesis, the perfection of osmosis! No pumping, heaving, killing, chewing, gulping, choking or eructing. A tree has no moving parts.'

"I say to him, 'All I know is I'm afraid to even go see my sons for fear I'll come back and you'll be a headline. What about those two old women who got murdered in this neighborhood in the last six months?'

"'Parasites,' he mutters, and I think he means me. 'Crawling, stinging, burrowing vermin. Shake them off. Dandruff and lice. A cocker spaniel. Who comes yapping to lick your sores with its acidic little tongue.'" She gave me a hard look. "When I was growing up," she said, "if you called a woman a dog, you were doing her serious harm. And also, of course, he knows I don't like to sleep alone. I used to wake in the night, even when the boys were little, to check them for breathing. When they were gone, I used to lie awake sure something had happened to them. I would wake him when it became too much, and he was the kindest man in the world when he wanted to be. 'Be still,' he's say. 'Be still and it will pass.'

"But that side of him, it's gone. When he was home with pneumonia, as soon as he began to recover, it started all over again, the ripping up newspapers and shouting."

I said, "Why don't you divorce him? Or just leave? Why do you stay?"

"Ah," she said, "That's the question, isn't it? I've bought tickets. The first time he called me a dog. I've made plans to go visit the boys, at least for a week or two and think over next steps. But a person gets in the habit of care taking. For me, it started early, with babies and then my parents. For the first three months, I was always making him lunches and bringing him flashlights and jackets, but he would lope off when he saw me coming and hide. I always found his hiding places. In December, though, he didn't come home for three nights in a row, and we were having steady sleet and cold rain, and that was when I found him shivering with fever and had to take him to the emergency room and he had pneumonia.

"I thought he was going to die then. I thought he wanted to die, and God help me maybe I wanted it too. But he improved, he came home. He started reading the papers. One day he picked up the radio and threw it out the window. It's a wonder we didn't get arrested both of us. When he started going out again, I was ready. I said to myself, This time I'm leaving.

"But this morning, on his way out the door, he stopped and turned around and his eyes were perfectly round like he was seeing something terrible. And he said very softly, 'Am I losing it?'

"I was so sick of him, I said,'Losing what? What are you talking about?'

"'My mind,' he said. 'Am I losing my mind?'

"And that was all it took, all of a sudden, I knew. I knew I was staying. I said, 'Yes, I believe you are.' And he just nodded his head and went out, and I had a cup of tea, and I looked at my travel brochures, and I looked at the pictures of our sons and their families, and I became more and more sure. That I wasn't leaving. Now do you understand?"

I shook my head no.

"I'm going to stay with him tonight," she said, putting the thermos and things back in the bag, pointing at the plastic shopping bags, which I saw now were fat because each one had a sleeping bag in it.

"You're going to sleep in the park too?"

"Oh, I don't know. We may not stay. I'm going to be a tree with him for a while. Anyhow, with two of us, and all the equipment, I expect someone from the park or the police will come." She stood up and hoisted the bags.

"Do you need help?"

"Not at all," she said. "I'm off to hear how the tree is superior to us miserable mammals."

85

I said, "Maybe he needs to be hospitalized– "

"Eventually. Maybe both of us. Or maybe we'll find a way for both of us actually to turn into trees. That might be the best ending."

Claribel Queen of Tunis and Antonio the Usurper of Milan

Claribel Queen of Tunis and Antonio the Usurper of Milan

Berber girls jangling with bracelets ride into the marketplace of Tunis and race in circles until their fathers and brothers catch up and herd them away, marry them off, hide their faces. But out on the desert, my spies tell me, the girls never stop riding. Some say they cook and give birth on horseback. I yearn to see them in the desert, but that would dishonor my Lord of Tunis, so I depend on my spies and eunuchs for information.

My spies told me about the white haired Italian galley slave who was shouting from a port hole that he once preserved the honor of the Queen of Tunis. Of course I sent them to buy him, expecting a desperate madman who might entertain us for a while, but when they brought him to me, there was no mistaking the face, no matter how white the hair and how sunken and brown the cheeks. He fell to his knees and kissed my toes and ankles: "Claribel Claribel God has been merciful to this great sinner! Of all the women and men on this earth there is none I would rather belong to!"

He worked his tongue into the crevices between my toes, but no one of my little realm of wives, eunuchs, and priests saw because of his shock of hair.

I said, "God is great. This old Italian eunuch is an ancient retainer from my father's house in Naples. Give him some clothes and something eat and he will recount his adventures for us."

Of course, as soon as he was refreshed and wearing linen robes, it was evident that he was neither especially old nor a servant. And the ones who bathed him had seen how much of a eunuch he was. He was a good storyteller, though; he held our attention through the whole evening with an incredible tale of adventures on an enchanted island and capture by pirates. The little wives and eunuchs and even my Italian priests gathered so tightly around him that the air became close and I had to chastise them till they moved back to a respectful distance.

When the pillows and rugs were finally taken up, and my people were gathered in little groups to talk about what they'd heard, I called him to my divan and had him sit at my feet. I said, "Antonio, if I'm to keep you, you'll have to become a true eunuch or else a priest."

He petted my foot as if it were a little animal. He did this brazenly, in full sight of the others, and with such assurance that everyone seemed to assume this was what Italian slaves did for their ladies.

He said, "Ah Princess, you cannot know. You cannot imagine. In the galleys we had nothing like this foot and nothing like your pretty, pretty boys who will never grow beards. It is wonderful to be tempted again. But I have decided to retire from the world, or perhaps to preach remorse and repentance."

"If I allow you," I said.

He kissed my foot. "Or I can stay here."

"No," I said, "You would corrupt the court. I'll be forced to free you."

"As you will, my lady."

I thought about what he had said. "No, Antonio, you'll never retire from the world. Not with your taste for pretty children and sending your enemies out to sea in leaky boats."

"My brother forgave me for what I did before we left the island," he said. "And the priests say great things are possible to great sinners."

I watched him carefully now because the smile was the same as always, the broad mouth that has tasted everything, eyes that narrow but don't close. I wondered what he really wanted. A passage back to Italy, of course, so he could resume his natural business of intrigue. His brother the right Duke of Milan had forgiven him, he said.

"I was the only one the pirates took," he said. "I suspect that was your Uncle Sebastian punishing me for my sins. I think I'll go and preach to Sebastian to mend his ways."

"Antonio," I said, "The only thing you ever believed in was the corruption of everybody."

"Except you, princess. You wanted to have a crusade against the infidel instead of marrying him, remember?"

I kicked him in the ribs. Had he become simple-minded to say such a thing in this place?

He displayed his teeth, one of the canines was missing. "Corruption is the message, little princess. I want to preach to Sebastian and to my brother Duke Prospero. Shave your head and come with me. You once wanted to run away with me. We'll preach salvation in Italy."

I laughed gaily so my husband's spies–who are in many cases the same ones I pay–would be sure to see that the remark is a joke. "I understand you now. You think you've found power greater than being a duke. I had been about to ask you if you would do it over again if you knew what was coming to you, if you would save me again. But of course you would since you are to become a saint."

"Come with me to Italy."

Oh I laughed and laughed. I would never leave Tunisia now anyhow– what would my enemies do to my sons? Besides, I have my little realm here in the women's quarters. I am judge of all their quarrels and suits.

And yet I sometimes imagine myself walking barefoot on the pink marble of my father's court at Naples with Antonio smiling at my side: Repent! I shout and point. Repent, you who sold a little girl to the Mussulman! I can smell the gardens and hear the plash of the fountain where I slept the last night before my marriage. I imagine doing this with no spies and no disguise, and with the hills of my childhood in the corner of my eyes.

Antonio always brought excitement when he came.

On his first visit to Naples when I was eleven, he was the most beautiful man I had ever seen. His hair already had a streak of white, and his clothes were white, too, with a little silver and gold top-stitching. He brought me and my brother Ferdinand a toy rabbit hutch in the perfect likeness of a Roman villa with colonnades and windows and views of vineyards and pagan temples. This was a kingdom for us to rule, said the silver prince from Milan, and I thought he was looking into the deepest heart of me as he said it. When he came back for his visit the next year, all of us ladies young and old were in love with him.

We gave him masques and hunts and banquets and told him how noble he was and how he would make a finer duke of Milan than old Prospero who so they said did nothing but blacken good Venetian glass in his search for the philosopher's stone. Even my father and Uncle Sebastian who usually complained about expenses spared no pains for Antonio. People attributed the open purse to Uncle Sebastian's being as smitten with Antonio as the women were.

Personally, I liked best the rumor that they were going to make an alliance with Milan by marrying me to him.

Sometime toward the end of the second visit, though, the freshness wore off. It seemed that Antonio had run out of white linen and silver thread. He was as witty as ever and as good at devising games and excuses for parties, and there was no question that the court of Naples was like a funeral when he wasn't with us, but we all knew that Sebastian had finally had his way with him. My ladies said that they wouldn't have minded his having a taste for pretty boys, but to love an old wartbeard like Uncle Sebastian was unconscionable. It may have been a case of sour grapes, too, because Sebastian would have poisoned any lady who diverted Antonio even for a night. So the ladies joked and called him Sebastian's little wife behind his back, and I silently marked the scoffers, vowing that one day I would be sovereign and I would string them up by their toe joints and set falcons at their eyes. I would marry Antonio and he would explain that all this playing at love with Uncle Sebastian had been a way of saving himself until I reached womanhood.

Antonio wore a chain of amethysts and a doublet of quilted velvet the night before his great coup. He danced with all the ladies, in spite of Sebastian, and I waited my turn, refusing to dance with anyone else, whispering to myself the lines of a sonnet I had written for him. "His mouth as cruel as the infidel's sword/ That scimitar cuts me with every word." When he came to me his face and hair were as bright as a ship sailing into the sunset. He bowed and took my hand to lead me to the figure, but I said, "Take me to Milan with you." I wanted to be his slave, I said, to hide in his saddlebags or cover my head with a hood and be his hunting bird. I'd be his bitch dog and sleep at his feet.

He walked me onto the terrace and I remember the moon making white flames on his face: the leap of his ambition and mine. When he kissed my forehead, I took it as a sign and clasped my arms around him, almost knocking us both over the balustrade. But I couldn't feel his flesh, only the hard carbuncles of his jewels and mine holding us apart.

"Princess, princess," he said. "You wouldn't want to go to Milan with me if you knew what I am going to do there."

"Whatever you do, I'll do it too."

"But I am death to little princesses, Claribel."

"Kill me then!"

He was thinking of his brother's little daughter whom he would soon push out to sea in the leaking boat along with her father. But I thought everything was a metaphor.

"Perhaps I will take you to bed one day, Princess. Perhaps when I'm Duke of Milan we'll join Milan and Naples between our sheets. Would you wait for me, how ever long until I become duke?"

"I don't care if you're only the Duke's brother."

"It might not be such a long wait. I'm not worth much as I am."

I became tongue tied wanting to say yes yes I'd wait forever and at the same time no no he could never be worth more than he was right now, and while I was sputtering and catching my breath, a shadow crossed the terrace and looked upon us; heavier and blacker than a shadow; it was Uncle Sebastian with his choking voice of anger.

"What are you doing out here with her?"

Antonio kept me in the crook of his arm and I thought that now we would make our declaration and I would nestle against him forever.

"Claribel and I are plotting. I've asked her to marry me when I become duke. I've told her everything and I'm waiting for an answer."

"You told her– "

"Yes!" I shouted at last. "I'll wait as long as you say. I'll wait till Doomsday!"

Sebastian's big hand came out of the dark at me and I dodged what I thought would be a slap, but he caught my chin tightly between his thumb and finger and pulled me away from Antonio. "You've been kissing her. Why are you doing this to me?"

They talked to each other above the level of my head.

"Maybe I want to be the man tonight."

"Whatever you say. It's all the same to me."

Antonio said, "Stay here, Princess. This is the beginning of your wait."

At first I refused to believe the reports of what happened in Milan. That in the dead of night Antonio had murdered Prospero's bodyguard and hustled the old duke and his little daughter out to sea in a boat with no rudder. If he wanted to be duke so much, I thought, why not challenge the old duke to a sword fight? But perhaps the whole business was malicious gossip, or perhaps most disturbing of all, Antonio had made his actions appear indefensible in order to test me! I believed in Antonio, but because he appeared ruthless to the world, I pretended to be ruthless too and wore black hoods and scarves and stared impolitely when people addressed me. I wanted everyone to look at me and be reminded of him, and when they saw him, to speak of me: She is still waiting for you, they would say, she wears the colors of dark deeds in the nights. And thus one day he would come for me and explain his real reasons and what really happened and we would all dress in silver and gold again.

Meanwhile someone had to tend to Naples while my father bred dogs and hawks, and Sebastian came back. There were those who said Antonio had cast him off, and he certainly snarled and stomped around the court. He and I were like a couple of carrion eaters skulking in the arcades of a charnel house. Neither one of us ever crossed an open space if we could find a dim passageway around. I would have done better, though, if I had stayed out of his way because it was Sebastian of course who thought up the project of marrying me to one of the infidel emirs in order to gain new trading concessions for Naples. It took him two years to complete an agreement with my Lord of Tunis: a dowry, the trade concessions, weddings in first Italy and then Tunisia, an arrangement for me to practice my religion. When they actually began to prepare the trousseau and outfit the ships, I sent a message to Milan: "They are sending me to Africa. Don't wait any longer." I think I expected Antonio to come and snatch me with a raiding party. Let there be a war, I thought. Let them raze Naples. I had been despicably treated here. I would build a new Naples and be queen and Antonio my king.

But when Antonio finally did come, it was as a wedding guest. They had set me on a little dais to receive my gifts, and there crossing the hall, wearing red, was Antonio with this well-turned calves and unwarlike smile. He knelt and kissed my fingertips. "So, Princess Claribel, you thought better of waiting after all."

I was shocked. "You didn't get my message?"

He glanced around the room, his smile never wavering, then looked straight into my face. "A message? From you Princess? To me?"

I was at once relieved and overcome by the strain of having to declare myself again. It did not occur to me that he might be lying. "I want you to take me away now. We can't wait any longer, don't you see? The infidel has already landed his ships!"

"The King of Tunis wouldn't like being cheated of his bride."

"We should have a crusade against the infidel, not a wedding!"

"A crusade over you, my little Helen?"

"Antonio, you can't believe I've been faithful to you or you would not make jokes."

"I believe you've been faithful. But what evidence did you ever have that I would be?"

This, I thought, is the last test. If it were not a test — My wedding clothes creaked around me and it took all the strength of my legs to rise. "If you mean that, then I am going to say good-bye." It was so clear there in front of my eyes, what I had to do, that I thought he had to see it too. The watch tower, I stand on the catwalk in the wind waiting for the sound of him running up the shaft to save me from jumping.

He kissed my hand and backed away.

I began to fall towards the ladies and gentlemen in red and green lining the walls like gentlefolk in a tapestry and when I tried to run they came out of the walls and crowded around me as if I were already dead.

"Her bodice is too tight," they said. "Is it here time of month?"

They carried me to my private apartments and gave me some wine, and when I revived I began to spill wine and oil and perfume on my new dresses and I smashed the empty bottles into the mirrors. I pinched and kicked the ladies who tired to stop me. My red cloud of fury became too heavy that the very weight of it slowed me and caused me to sleep. While I slept they removed all dangerous clasps and needles from my room and cleared out the valuables except for a few strands of pearls..

Black clouds had collected around the sunset and the sound of trumpets meant that the Tunisians were processing to the city gates. I let them massage me and feed me hot milk when I woke and they told me this was pretty and that was pretty and my pink toenails and my eyelashes and wouldn't the king of Tunis think he was the luckiest man in the world when he had seen me as they were seeing me now?

That night the women camped all over my rooms, on the divans, in the window seats, two in the bed with me and three others on the floor wrapped in cloaks. But since the rooms were quilted with human bodies, they thought I was safe and drank too much and slept too soundly. But I didn't sleep at all. I lay listening to the sounds of laughing

97

and music coming from Uncle Sebastian's quarters. Ever since I became old enough for my maidenhood to be a valuable commodity on the international market, Sebastian had kept me close to his quarters.

I climbed off the bed at the foot and quietly draped the robes of pearls around my waist and hips and wrapped myself in a dressing cape. I had in mind that the cape would wave as I leaped from the tower. I climbed out the window and walked through the garden, taking my time, pausing at the fountain. In the back of my mind I think I knew I wasn't going to make it to the tower— too many guards, too many wakeful revelers. I was not as sorry as I pretended either, and when I heard the sound of hurrying feet on the walk, I hid behind the fountain, and had a new idea.

It was my littlest page, panting as he trotted along. I grabbed him from behind and squeezed the back of his neck. Such a baby, he whined and moaned, so young he believed me when I hissed that I'd been waiting out here especially to catch him. "How much does he pay you?" I whispered. "How much does Sebastian pay you to go and do bad things at his parties? I've seen you in the morning when you're so tired you put my slippers on the wrong feet. Don't you know what we do to pages who try and serve two masters?"

"I never," he sniveled. "I never did."

"Maybe I won't punish you this time. You're so stupid you probably don't even know enough to get money from Sebastian. Tell me, do you expect the Duke of Milan to be there tonight? Is that a yes? Well, you're lucky then. Because I have to speak to him privately. And your only chance is to bring him to me right now. Do you understand?"

It made me feel almost cheerful to see him scurry off. After a while Antonio and my page came out on the terrace. I smoothed pearls at my waist and retraced the cape. The page was pointing towards me, but they were in the pink party light and I was in the dark. Antonio laid a hand kindly on the page's head.

"Well, princess," he said as he approached the fountain. "Well well"

I jerked the boy from under his hand. "Go home. You're safe for now, but go home and go to bed and don't let me catch you at Sebastian's again."

"You're very careful about the upbringing of your pages."

"No one takes the children in hand. Someone should be taking care of all the children around this court."

Antonio took a vial out of his sleeve. "Pardon me, I have to clear my head."

I pulled his free hand under my cape and touched it to the pearls, pressed his knuckles into my bare waist.

"Ye Gods, Claribel, you're naked!"

"I know you don't like women."

He put away the vial and opened my cape to look at me. "I like whatever is beautiful of its kind."

"Then sleep with me. Take me to your bed or take me here under the fountain. I'll never ask you for another favor."

"If I slept with you tonight, we might neither one live to ask or grant favors."

"I don't care if I live or die. But the infidel won't buy damaged goods."

"Ah, and I'm to do the damaging?" Very slowly he rearranged my pearls. Each little cold jewel touched my skin in a new place, but not his fingers. Antonio seemed slow and time was passing in palpable spheres like the pearls under his fingers. "Don't you understand that this marriage has nothing to do with women and men? It has to do with trade? You are going to save your father and Sebastian from the usurers."

"Why can't they hang the usurers?"

"Not a bad idea. I'll keep it in mind for when I come into debt." He patted my hair. "Poor little goose. Fattened on prunes and almonds all these years and now the feast day is coming."

"Are you going to do it for me?"

"Let's sit down her on the steps to the fountain and consider it."

"If you won't, I'm going to the guards. I'll go from one to the other until I find someone who will and if they are all cowards, I'll do it myself on a sword."

He sat, pulled me down. "Sit on my lap and we'll light a pipe."

"You aren't going to do it, are you?"

"Take off your cape and I'll open my shirt so we can keep each other warm." He settled me against his naked chest and covered us both with the cape and began taking things out of his clothes, a small brass pipe, silk bag of brown sulphurous balls, a flint. Don't think I was fooled; I could tell he was putting me off. I could tell by the deliberate way he shifted me about on his chest while he filled and lighted the pipe. But I could also tell I wasn't going to run from him. This was after all what I had wanted for years, to be held by Antonio, and he was holding me. I could smell his tobaccos and his incenses and his wines. A fog rose up in me and blended with what we were smoking, and bit by bit the vault of the sky was completely obscured. The vault shifted once, inverted so that it became an abyss at my feet and I clung to Antonio for dear life and called his name and he got us more to smoke and the abyss was secured in one position and we ate some little dried truffles that made us rest again.

Flares came out of the darkness once and I cried for Antonio and he told the flares to stand back, he was taking care of everything.

I woke toward dawn and pulled the cape over us. The sky was hidden in a blue gray mist and I shook him awake. "Are you going to do it?"

He shook his head no. Uncle Sebastian's guards stood in a circle around us at a little distance.

"Then you better give me something else to eat," I said, and with his eyes still closed, he found me another dried truffle. After I ate it, I looked into his face, his closed eyes and broad smile, and beyond the mist with nothing to focus my eyes on, and all through the whole wedding, through the sea voyage and through the other wedding too, Antonio provided me with mists and fogs so that I never really woke up until I was the Queen of Tunis and Antonio had long been shipwrecked with the others on the magic island.

Miss Topsy

Miss Topsy

So thoroughly efficient was Miss Ophelia in her conscientious endeavor to do her duty by her élève, that the child rapidly grew in grace and in favor with the family and neighborhood.
– Harriet Beecher Stowe, final pages of Uncle Tom's Cabin

Miss Ophelia on her death bed in summer

I take my rest in the afternoons, in the extra chamber, not on the cot in our room. I choose to nurse her at night when she is most afraid. I don't sleep much, never deeply. We are all waiting. How will she pass over? What will we feel without her? Who will I be then? She and I have been two strands of a braid, and the third strand, that long-gone angel Miss Eva.

For many years we planned that I would become a missionary after she went, but she stopped mentioning it after a while, and I am no youthful voyager anymore; I approach my half century. Sometimes I imagine, with more likelihood of its coming to pass, that I will go back to New Orleans wearing a great brimmed sun hat, and no one know me unless I tell, and even then, it would be so fantastic they wouldn't believe.

Most likely, I'll stay here, attending our church, singing, praying, putting in a garden, making jelly, keeping an eye on the Irish girl. Sleeping in our double bed. But I think I shall wear more yellow when Ophelia is gone. New Orleans yellow of banana and fragrant jasmine, Vermont yellow of sunflowers. In the end, Miss Ophelia and I reconciled on almost every point except my preference for yellow. "Jungle rising up in you!" she would cry. "Savage tiger eyes!" And I would remind her that tigers are native to the Indian subcontinent, not to Africa. "No, Miss Ophelia," I would say, "it is only my natural born desire to ornament my natural born color the way God meant it to be ornamented." In our battles, the soft word and calm mien always triumphed.

I never did become tractable the way Miss Ophelia led the ladies of the Bible Society to believe. Those ladies who thought they were investing in stock for the Great African Missionary Plan. They intended to save the Heathen and have one less black girl in Vermont by a single act of frugal charity. They bought me my first white dress and my first whalebone corset.

My Stays

We do not take naps, Miss Ophelia and I, nor do we loosen our stays during the day. On the other hand, we don't do housework in the afternoons, in case anyone should drop by. A lady is not to be found on her hands and knees scrubbing when folks call, says Miss Ophelia. In the afternoon, a lady does a bit of fancy work, or reads. Miss Ophelia prefers Milton or the Bible. I usually open the *Collected Plays of William Shakespeare* but spend much of my time gazing at the mountains. They are a spectacle for me after all these years: so much air out there and our white pines reaching up into it: enormities of tree and sky and mountain. I sit without moving, to all appearances still and staid, but I am growing larger and larger, filling the empty space, becoming a natural phenomenon

I began as a city creature, accustomed to courtyards and streets and back halls where I slept on pallets made of cast-off clothes. What I knew of Nature was lush flower-ing cultivated things: pomegranate trees, oranges, geraniums, Arabian jasmine and native. Spiky old aloes like prickly wizards. But these were all contained, walled in, not sublime like the Vermont mountains. Up here, in the cold and the spaciousness, I had to grow heavier, and I needed my stays.

Let me say here and now that I have no regrets. I am proud to be a New Englander, proud of my straight back and my hands that stay in my lap neither gesturing nor touching my face. Proud of my education and my position in the community. I do not pine for my heathen days. What would I have been in New Orleans? Fodder for flies, if I'd stayed as wicked as I was: beaten to death by some drunken master. In this house we are Abolitionists who have witnessed the depravities engendered by the Institution we wish to abolish. I would have been there at best a house servant, thieving what I could among my mistress's old silks and laces. Prey to the master and his acquaintance had I turned plump and pretty. Oh, far better New England freedom, dignity, Christianity. I praise the Lord and Miss Ophelia for the goodness that has befallen me, for the stays they have laced around me.

I praise her and value her, and have built my life around her, but as a teacher, Miss Ophelia's single purpose was to contain my wild energy. I did not particularly like her in the beginning, and she was at first repulsed by me. These New Englanders have their principles, but do not love easily. It was a long time before she learned to teach and I learned to learn.

In the end, we both succeeded. I am still a fantastic creature, but I know how to watch by a sick bed and how to sing hymns without rocking. How to perch my buttocks on little visiting chairs and how to pronounce each syllable and each letter of each word. It has become my work, my labor and my fancywork, to make no errors, to be as close and neat as a born New Englander.

But do not mistake me for an imitation. I am a real thing like nothing else. I am that fine, dignified, Christian colored lady, who was raised like a daughter by Miss Ophelia.

I regret nothing, except that she brought me to Vermont in winter.

Cold Times; My Cold

At first I ran like a wild thing, looking out windows, marveling. "Miss Ophelia," I cried, "Miss Ophelia, is I going to turn white from all this stuff?" But then I began to slow down like a steam engine deprived of fuel, to cough and finally to roll backwards and stop. They wrapped me in quilts, but wherever they laid me, I turned my face to gaze out the window at the whiteness. "Is that heaven?" I whispered. "Is that where Miss Eva is? Because if it is, I ain't going there nohow."

I was a funny little monkey, Miss Ophelia told me, even when I was in delirium.

How hard for her to see me, she said, not saved yet, failing before her eyes. Losing what bit of flesh I had, a dying child grey and dun where Miss Eva had been white and gold. Me with no wealth to dispense, no people to bless, no evangelist's message to convey to those left behind.

I don't remember being ill, but I remember that there was no color in that place. That the house, the people, the snowy land, were pale as death, marked with iron bars, tree branches, unsupple backs, and compressed thin lips. The fire grew smaller, and my fists turned to stones. The air, thin as a razor, scraped at my neck. I saw Miss Eva floating over the snowy fields, her feet never touching, her white garments waving, and she laughed like icicles and came and stood between me and Miss Ophelia and told me I was coming to see her soon.

"No I ain't!" I whispered, shivering. "No I ain't you cold devil girl!"

And kept shivering, burning up with fever and looking for something warm. In desperation, to save me, Miss Ophelia took me into her bed one night and stayed there the next day, with me fixed firmly against her bony old self in its flannel night gown. She held me firm as I shook and kept my head under the feather mattresses. On the second night, she put me under her night gown, face to her skin, faintly acrid and also spicy with the cinnamon she used in baking, and I nestled there in that darkness, and I could hear her stomach growl and her voice giving orders to the girl, pretending she was sick herself and that was why she had stayed in bed. The little monkey's fever was like a warming pan, she told them.

And I thought, I'm a warming pan, that's what I am.. I pictured myself iron hard with a glowing coals inside, and I nestled there, and was warm, and my fever broke, and I came out of the covers alive and strong, reborn from Miss Ophelia's body.

Our Work

Our work was the transmogrification of Topsy. We used to try and separate out who had changed what about me: I claimed that I was a quick study; she claimed to be a great teacher. "Think," she said, "of the cultivation of your accent."

"I have a musical ear," I said.

"But," she smiles just the slightest bit with her thin lips, those lips which always whiten long before she even knows herself she is in a passion. "Where would your mimic's ear have been without an accent to imitate?"

Coolness, natural to her, was the test of our reasoning. Coolness a gift she was born with, which brought out the heat in me, and I had to learn to bide my time and wait out my anger. I considered this stupendous effort of self-control a virtue. She called me cunning.

The paragon, the threat and promise of my childhood, of course, had been the White Angel. I can still hear Ophelia say, "Oh Topsy, wouldst thou have Miss Eva looking down from Heaven and see this?" This being the theft of a gingerbread nut or the stripping off of stockings to run barefoot.

"Don't you Thee me and Thou me," I would yell. "Don't you call me that, Miss Ophelia."

Because, let there be no mistake about it, Miss Ophelia knew how to torment her naughty Topsy as well as Topsy knew how to torment Miss Ophelia. Maybe better in the beginning, when I was so cold and so eager for Miss Ophelia to love me more than little Eva. I knew in my heart that I wanted the stockings to stay on, the ginger-bread nuts to be requested politely, the nappy hair be oiled smooth.

"I don't know much about saints, not being a Papist myself," said Miss Ophelia, "but I believe Eva was the most perfect Christian it has ever been my privilege to know." We talked all day long as we mended, crocheted, made tatting.

"I believe," said I, older than when she first held her up as a model to me, "I believe that our Miss Eva was too good for this world."

"Well that's true for a surety," said Miss Ophelia, biting a thread.

"In fact," said I, "I believe that, had she survived to adulthood, she could not possibly have been an angel."

"A different kind of angel," said Miss Ophelia. "Angel of her husband's House as she was of her Father's."

"Yes," I say, "Of course she would have sent her babies off to their colored Mammy– even the finest Southern ladies are too high strung to nurse their own– "

Miss Ophelia stirs in her chair as if something itched her, but I can't stop, I feel I have cornered my prey, will throttle the Angel once and for all. "It's not that she'd have a choice, Miss Ophelia, she'd have all those fittings for all those white dresses. She had to look like a picture when she was doing good– not that I blame her, Miss Ophelia, I like a good watered silk myself, as you know. But you wouldn't want people to start thinking that good wasn't pretty– you wouldn't want people to start thinking that goodness isn't clean and white– "

Miss Ophelia's lips like two sticks of chalk rolling together. "She was a better person than you or I could ever hope to be."

"She was a sugar tit," I said, and Miss Ophelia stopped just short of slapping my face, and I thought Oh where have we gotten to this time? And yet, better Miss Ophelia tight with rage and smelling of apple vinegar, her sweat and her armpits. I have never been able to abide sweetness.

On another occasion I told her, "I have decided to change my name."

Ophelia sighed. "It never was a proper Christian name. Do you know, I never liked mine either – that Shakespearean creature who goes mad for love and commits suicide. I always imagined myself as more of a Portia."

I said, "I will call you Portia, if you will call me Jasmine."

"Jasmine!" she cried out. "Jasmine! Why not Orchid or Forget-me-not! Why not Juno or Jezebel!"

"It has a fragrance," I say, gratified by the way her eye flashes and her lip curls. "It creates an atmosphere!"

"Not the one I raised you in!"

To which I reply, "Perhaps your influence is less over me than you like to pretend."

"I admit," said Miss Ophelia, "that I have had the Devil's own time getting anything resembling a Christian out of you. I admit that you are still half a wicked urchin from the streets of that three-quarters foreign city!"

"Perhaps I should have stayed," I say. "Perhaps I would have become a market woman with my own little children playing in my skirts..." I strike her in a vulnerable spot here: she thinks herself guilty of keeping me from the fathers of the children I never had.

"Children!" she cries. "Market! You would have been on the market, not in the market. Not fish and chickens on sale but your own body and soul! Sometimes I am appalled that you joke about such things."

"I'm free," I say. "I don't owe you, do I? I can say what I please?"

"You are free," she says grimly.

"Ophelia," I say, "I am free, but I freely owe it to you."

"Why do you tease me?" she asks, and I can't answer, not even to tell the truth, which is that I feel lonely even when I am with her. We have such different gaits, to be yoked together.

Miss Ophelia Lets Go

But now Miss Ophelia is old and so many things still unsettled between us. Some angers never dissolved, we only walked around them to join hands again, and now the enormity of my loneliness as I realize she is leaving me. I never admitted it till an evening in the spring mud season when there was still snow on half the yard and the girl and I were in the kitchen peeling potatoes. I looked up and saw her; she had gone out into the back yard, her skirt tucked up into her apron and her feet stone naked. She was

112

running in a little circle, stepping in the cold dense mud, wading in the snow. We went out at once, and she ran from us, full of joy, daring us to catch her.

We had to carry her inside that time, her old chicken bone body giving a twist and chuckle every so often. "Who's the monkey now, Topsy?" she asked me. We wrapped her in shawls and quilts and set her near the stove and boiled water and put her feet in a bucket. We loosened her stays; her hairpins had already come out.

I massaged her feet to get the circulation going. Those perfectly hairless thin old legs, the skin shiny, one toenail turned black and crooked. Except for that nail, as pretty and fine boned and white as Miss Eva's. Her ankles, perhaps, a little swollen, but only enough to smooth out the line, make them seem fuller. She sang songs, like her namesake, her mind wandering, while the Irish girl made tea and whiskey and I chafed those feet, those ankles and legs, as if the strength of my hands would return her to herself.

She tucked her chin down small and turned her eyes up huge. "Have I been a bad girl?"

"Yes, Miss Ophelia," I say, very formal in front of the girl, but with my heart beating harder and faster because I see it now, her going down, my loneliness. "Yes, Miss Ophelia, you have been *méchante*."

She laughs and laughs. "Topsy, Topsy. Yes, yes. Who's the monkey now?"

So be it, I think. She is to be my little girl now and I her mother. It is only that so much was left undone. So little time that we were face to face. And no other human being who knows me. But I say, like a good guardian, "Yes, Ophelia, and if you are a monkey now, then we had best hide our knitting yarn."

She nods her head so seriously and bangs her heels against the chair. "Yes, and I'll kick over the pickle barrel and drop the preserves and the vases too."

And this is the way it has been. When the ladies come to visit and we've had a mess, I say, Miss Ophelia has been naughty, my friends. I am sorry for the disorder.

It is perhaps just as well that she is going out as a naughty child, because it would be terrible to see her in fear for her soul: "What have I made of you?" she used to groan. "You should have had children, I am a monster of licentiousness."

"I touched you first," I would say.

And she groan again: "One little black ewe lamb and what have I done?"

"You were never my shepherd," I said. "I am not a sheep. You are Portia and I am Jasmine."

"Tell me a story," she says. "Make me forget. Tell me about the spice air."

I breathe in deeply of Miss Ophelia's vinegar, I feel the winds of hot June in New Orleans as we rock back and forth together. We are transported, the wind under our dresses, the sun on our feet.

And after a while, she says, "Are we wicked, Topsy?"

And I say, "How can we be wicked when you freed me and I am free?"

A Vision of Miss Eva

That was always my answer, but I ask the question for myself now, as she lies dying. What was good and what was wicked, or was none of it neither or all of it both?

I lie in the bed sweating, and, in my desire, I make up another story for her. Miss Eva comes from Heaven to speak with me. She has grown tall, as you'd expect of an angel, but she has never filled out, is still skinny as a consumptive, pale as a specter.

114

"Hello Topsy," she says, swaying and wavering like a sheer curtain the wind draws in and out.

"People call me Miss Topsy these days," I say, just to be sure she doesn't get the jump on me.

She smiles wanly: but everything about her is wan. She says, "What if I call you Topsy and you call me Eva."

So I say, "All right, Eva. I suppose you enjoy Heaven, Eva. I suppose it's just the kind of thing you'd like."

"Oh I do, Topsy. Heaven is a wonderful place."

"Lots of sitting on benches and singing hymns?"

"Lots of singing," she nods.

I want to find out if they think us wicked in Heaven. I come at it obliquely, work around my objective. "Miss Ophelia's passing over soon. She has been a good woman."

Eva sways and smiles.

I say, "But me, I don't know if I'll ever make it. I never did get as bleached out and good as everyone wanted of me."

"Well Topsy," says Eva, "I don't know if I should tell you or not, but Heaven is wonderful, like they all say, but it isn't like they all say. It's much more lively." And her long arms like wands make little circles in the air. "They expect more– cutting up and hijinks– than I ever would have guessed. It was quite a surprise to me really. I'd been lying around on pillows too long, I guess. I wish I'd been more fun-loving back then, like you."

"Ho!" I say. "Fun-loving welts in the back of your knees? You may have learned to cut up in Heaven, but you haven't learned good sense."

"But Topsy, you and Ophelia together– you were free."

A warm bath of well-being comes over me and I find myself looking away from her silly spectral whiteness, but I still want to hear her voice. "It wasn't a sin then, how we came to love each other? You're sure it wasn't a sin? I don't ask for myself so much as for her."

115

Eva said, "Tell Ophelia this for me, Topsy. Whisper it in her ear. Tell her I'm not as energetic as I could be. Tell her I need livening up. She'll find it easier to come if she knows she has someone to take care of when she gets here."

As she departs, Eva brushes me with her sheer hand and the folds of her skirt.

"Who will take care of me?" I cry.

And then I remember that I had sobbed at Eva's deathbed too: I loved Eva before I loved Ophelia. Oh Eva, I think. Oh Ophelia. What will be left for me?

A storm is coming out of the East. I turn my face to it. We'll watch the storm together, I think, and I'll tell Ophelia the story. It will build her up for the hijinks in heaven.

A Note On the Sources

The sources of these stories are mostly well-known. For example, Miss Topsy is the free, grown-up slave girl from *Uncle Tom's Cabin*. "The Great Wolf" and "Martha, Sister of Lazarus" come from the King James translation of the Protestant Christian Bible, and other stories are from myth and tales and legends. "The Adventure of Dunzyad, Scheherezade, and the King" is one of these, as is "Baucis and Philemon #3." In writing the latter, I was thinking of both Ovid and Jonathan Swift's poetic versions.

Some of the stories I made up from whole cloth. Examples of this would be "Her Statue" and "Legend of the Locust Root." I wrote one story, "Sermon of the Younger Monica," after reading the *Confessions* of Saint Augustine, who never gives the name of his concubine.

Finally, in Shakespeare's late play *The Tempest* there is brief mention of Claribel, who never appears on stage. Her wedding is the reason for the sea journey that results in the shipwreck and events on Prospero's island. My inspiration for "Claribel Queen of Tunis and Antonio the Usurper of Milan" was a 1974 production of the play at the New York Shakespeare Festival with Christopher Walken as Antonio.

CPSIA information can be obtained at www.ICGtesting.com
Printed in the USA
BVOW050838141011

273601BV00001B/4/P